A Summer to Remember

by Bonnie Towne

To my husband, Alyn

Cover photo by Dale R. Briggs

One

EVERYBODY loves my sister Janie, including me. But sometimes I hate her. She is a year younger than I am, and she's more popular. I really hate to admit that. But I guess I should face facts.

I envy almost everything about Janie. I used to lie in bed at night and wish that I were Janie. I wished that I had been born second and that she were Margaret, the older sister.

What is it about Janie, her looks? That's what boys notice right away. Janie and I look a lot alike. We both have light brown hair and clear blue eyes. But Janie's eyes seem friendlier, and her hair feathers back perfectly. My hair just kind of hangs there in its own waves that stick out in the most peculiar spots. I'm five feet, five inches tall, and Janie is one inch shorter. We both weigh 115 pounds. But she looks curvy in the right places, and I feel terribly fat at times. Janie's legs are slim, and mine are heavier. Mom says

I take after her side of the family, which is my bad luck.

In the boy department, Janie is tops. I think she could get any boy in the whole world to like her and ask her out. All my friends agree. They say Janie has more boyfriends than any other girl in school. It's a little embarrassing to be the older sister of such a popular girl. Here I am sixteen years old, and I've only had two real dates.

Last year I went to the Homecoming Dance with Howie Jordan, whose mother is my mom's best friend. Our mothers practically arranged the whole thing. Howie is all right as far as boys go, but he seemed as bored with me as I was embarrassed to go out with him. My other date was with Bill Creamer, a good friend. He and I have taken all the computer courses at school. And we both spend a lot of time writing programs on the computer. We only went out because we discovered we both like horror movies.

With Janie it's more like planning her social calendar. It's a rare Saturday night that she doesn't have a choice of boys to go out with. Sometimes she has two dates in one day—one to the beach in the afternoon and another at night. What is it that attracts the boys so fast? I have to know, because I have just met the most fabulous guy I've ever seen in my entire life. If I ever wanted to be Janie, it was when I met Frost Duvall.

It was just three and a half hours ago that Frost came into my mom's shell shop. And I'm sure I'm in love. What else would make my stomach flip, my heart lurch, my face red, and my hands turn to ice?

I had to absolutely force myself to speak to him. Well, actually all I did was answer him. He didn't know the difference between an olive shell and a cowrie. So he asked a lot of questions. Finally he got around to asking the kinds of questions I liked.

"Do you live around here?" he asked.

"Yes, I live on the island. This is my mom's shell shop," I said. I tried to smile like Janie does, but my face felt frozen.

"What do you do for entertainment?" He was looking at me with those big brown eyes.

"We go to the beach mostly," I stammered. "Sometimes we go into Fort Myers to see a movie."

"Well, I'll be seeing you," he said, and he left.

I didn't know what "I'll be seeing you" meant. Right away I wanted to tell Janie about Frost. But that would be the wrong thing to do. All I needed was to lose Frost to Janie before I even got to know him. I decided to keep him a secret for a little while.

We live on Sanibel Island. It can be really
dead here in the summer. Most of the
residents go to the mountains in North
Carolina. That leaves behind those of us who
can't afford to go anywhere. Everybody hates
how hot summer gets in southern Florida, but
we manage. My dad is a high school math
teacher in Fort Myers, and my mom runs a
shell shop year round. Dad sells real estate in
the summer. But some years he doesn't sell
much of anything—like this summer for
instance. He's been spending most of his time
hunting for shells for Mom's shop. Mom lets
Janie and me take turns running the shop so
we can earn our spending money. Mom always
says, You can't buy training like that! when we
have to do the boring work like dust a
thousand shells or scrub the floors after a
hundred tourists have tracked in sand all day.

"Why are you so quiet today, Margaret?"
Mom asked, as I drove her home after we
closed up the shop.

"No reason. I just don't have anything to
say." I had been thinking about Frost, but I
couldn't tell her that.

We pulled into the driveway of our cottage.
We used to live on the beach, but last year a
big construction firm built a seven story
condominium between us and the water. Now
we don't have a gulf view anymore. But it's

still only a short walk to the water. Dad says condominium living is the way of the future. People own their apartments and pay a fee to maintain a pool and the sea wall.

"Mom, when a person says 'I'll be seeing you,' does that mean they'll see you, or is it just an expression?" I asked when we reached the kitchen.

"It depends," Mom said. "Probably the person intends to see you. Why?"

"I just wondered." I headed for the room I share with Janie. What I wouldn't give for a room of my own. I'd hoped to slip out to the beach without seeing her. But there she was, painting her nails.

"Yuck, that stuff stinks," I said. The minute I'd said it, I wished I hadn't. Janie doesn't go around insulting people before she says hello.

"Sorry, Margaret, but I have a big date tonight with Allen Patten." Janie smiled sweetly.

"If a stranger asked you what you do around here for entertainment, what would you tell him?" I asked.

"There's Freddie's in Fort Myers for dancing. The best thing to do is look for a beach party if he's good looking."

Why hadn't I thought of that?

"Who wants to know about a party?" Janie asked.

"Nobody. I just wondered."

"I met the cutest boy on the beach today," Janie started. What I hate about Janie most is how she gushes over boys.

"He was so cute. He had dimples and blond, curly hair and lots of muscles," she went on. She was smiling into space. How I hated that look.

"I met a cute boy today myself. His name is Frost Duvall," I blurted.

"Oh, really? Tell me about him." Janie had her boy-sensing radar finely tuned.

"He has dark hair, wavy but not too curly, and muscles and a tan and big brown eyes." Why couldn't I keep quiet?

"Sounds interesting."

"You're not the only one who can meet boys," I said, hotly.

"Why, Margaret, I didn't even know you'd discovered boys. Don't get so excited," Janie said.

"Forget it," I snarled. "I just met him, that's all."

I changed into my swimming suit and escaped to the beach. Being alone on the beach is the best way to sort out my thoughts. I love to sit on the sand and watch the waves keep rolling up on the shore.

But today even the waves weren't helping. Since Janie was so much better at attracting boys, I had always pretended not to notice them. The truth is I like boys as much as she does. What girl doesn't? So I finally meet a cute boy, and I spill the whole story to Janie.

"Hey, I didn't think I'd see you again so soon." Frost sat down beside me on the sand.

"Well, hi." I couldn't believe it.

"Do you live around here?" he asked.

"You asked that before, but the answer is yes." I laughed.

He laughed, too. His face was wonderful when he laughed. His teeth were white and straight, and he had a nice smile.

"Want to go for a walk? You can show me how to hunt for those shells you were telling me about."

"Sure," I said, still finding it hard to believe this was real.

We were actually talking and walking, and I hadn't embarrassed myself yet. We stopped every so often to pick up shells. I rattled on about the shells since that's something I know about. When we got back to my towel, our hands were full of cat's paws, worm shells, and one king's crown.

The sun was beginning to set, turning the sky to shades of pink and coral. I had stopped being so self-conscious, and Frost and I were having a good time, almost like friends. Frost was so good-looking with his dark hair against the coral sky, I wanted to cry. I knew I was in love. And I knew my life would be changed forever, no matter what.

"I'll see you tomorrow," he said.

Frost left quickly. I stood there with my hands full of shells and stared at his tracks in the sand.

Two

I was glad it was Janie's day to work at the store. I wanted to rush out to the beach and wait for Frost. But if I went too early, he might think I was too anxious to see him. What would Janie do? She always flirted like crazy until a boy asked her out. Then she played a little more hard to get. But I wasn't as sure of myself as she was.

After Mom had asked me for the second time why I was fidgeting around the house, I headed for the beach. It was about ten o'clock.

Wow! Frost was waiting for me. My stomach lurched and I thought I was going to be sick. I tried to think of something to say all the way down the path. I wanted to be cool so he wouldn't find out how he affected me. But I just blurted out, "Hey, I'm glad you're here." I grinned at him like an idiot.

He grinned back and we didn't have any more trouble after that. When Frost was smiling at me, I felt in full control of being

11

sweet and cute and popular.

"There are some guys windsurfing in front of my condo," he said. "Want to walk down and watch them?"

"Sure," I said.

We walked slowly not noticing much except each other.

"Where are you from?" I asked.

"Orlando," Frost said. "My dad is in real estate. He's made a fortune in condo-conversions. We're spending the summer here because Dad is selling the units in the motel we're staying in."

I was a little intimidated by how easily he mentioned the word "fortune." But it only bothered me for a second. Having lots of money wasn't something I was caught up in. Maybe that was because I didn't have much money to be concerned about. Fortunately, I didn't have to ask him what a condo-conversion was. Converting motels or apartments to condominiums was pretty plopular in Florida.

"The only bad thing about Dad's work is we move all over the state. Mom wants to be with Dad," Frost said. "Sometimes I get tired of going to new schools."

"Gosh, I've lived in the same house all my life," I said.

"There they are," Frost said, pointing to the

windsurfers' brightly-colored striped sails.

We sat on the beach and watched the tanned surfers cling to the handlebars of their sails as their surfboards skimmed along the water. Sometimes it wasn't clear who was in charge, the sailors or the wind. When the boys came in for a rest, we went over to talk to them. Frost asked lots of questions. I stood there and listened. I would have never approached them by myself. There I was, Margaret Halton, who has problems with popularity, surrounded by four cute guys. If only Janie could have seen me.

"Where's a good place to have lunch?" Frost asked, after we watched the guys take their boardsails out again.

"I don't know. Any of the motels have sandwich shops." He took me by surprise.

"Want to have lunch with me?" He was so cute, just looking at him made my temperature rise five degrees.

"Sure," I said.

I didn't realize how hungry I was until we entered the sandwich shop of the Island Inn, one of the newer motels on the island. The cheapest thing on the menu was a hot dog, and it cost $3.75.

I never eat lunch out. I'm saving all my money for college. Ever since I can remember, Mom and Dad have told Janie and me how important college is, and how we were going to have to save for it. When Frost ordered a double cheeseburger and fries, I gulped and ordered a hot dog.

"I didn't realize this place was so expensive," I said.

"Don't worry about it." He grinned at me. "You haven't told me about yourself yet."

I didn't know what to say. I couldn't exactly confess my big problem was I was unpopular with boys. Like a complete idiot, I started telling him about my sister, Janie.

Just then I saw Nancy Reilly walking toward me. Nancy's one of my best friends, but she's probably the worst blabbermouth on the whole island.

"Hi, Margaret! What's new?" Nancy stared at Frost.

I introduced them. Now the whole town would know about Frost.

"Have you been to Freddie's yet?" Nancy asked.

"No, but Margaret's going to take me there," Frost said.

"You'll really like it. Go soon," Nancy said.

At least Nancy never gushes over boys the way Janie does, I thought. She just wants to be their friend.

"Well, I'll see you around," Nancy said.

"Do you care for dessert?" Our waitress

held up a menu. She handed it to Frost.

The thought of dessert after a $3.75 hot dog seemed very luxurious.

"What would you like, Margaret?" Frost asked.

"A hot fudge sundae," I said.

"Make that two," Frost said. "Do you go to school in Fort Myers?"

"Yes," I replied, and that got me going on school and how I took all the computer courses I could. Frost sure knew the right questions to ask.

The sundaes tasted as yummy as they looked. I didn't know which was better, eating a hot fudge sundae or being with Frost. It wasn't much of a contest. I knew I'd even give up hot fudge sundaes to be with Frost.

When we finished eating, we wandered over to the game room. Frost got a high score on a video game. I played so badly I was embarrassed. I convinced him I would rather watch him play.

"Why are you so serious? It's only a game," he said.

"Oh, I wasn't thinking about the game," I said.

"What were you thinking about?"

"That's classified top secret." It was so easy to be playful with him.

When he left me at my path, he gave my

arm a squeeze. At first I felt disappointed. Then I felt a rush of anticipation as I hurried up the path to my house. He had said he would see me tomorrow.

When I got to the porch I stopped. My heart dropped back down the steps. I had told Frost I would see him tomorrow, and I had to work. I was furious with myself for not remembering.

In our room Janie was playing the radio at screeching volume. "Shut that thing off," I shouted.

"Okay! Just take it easy." Janie smiled sweetly.

I glared at Janie. She looked gorgeous as usual. All I need, I thought, is for Frost to run into Janie tomorrow.

Three

I went to work in the rain. The sky was gray-blue, and the ocean was a deep blue-gray. I was in a gray funk because I could see Frost waiting for me on the beach and running into Janie instead. I called Nancy and told her what a predicament I had gotten myself into. As usual Nancy said for me not to worry. She always calmed me down.

The store was busy all day on account of the rain. When people can't go to the beach, they go shopping. It's a standard joke among the store owners to pray for rain.

When I got home I searched the house. "Where's Janie?" I asked Mom.

"Why she went to the movies. What's the matter?" Mom asked.

"Who did she go with?"

"She left a note saying she was going with some boy named Frost Duvall. She said you knew him."

"Yes, I know him." I went to my bedroom.

My stomach was lurching again, and I knew I would be sick. I lay on my bed and wished I could die. I wanted to call Nancy and tell her she was wrong, but I didn't have the heart for it. The rain beat down on the roof in a steady rhythm. I imagined Janie and Frost laughing and not even noticing it was raining.

I tried to think logically. I had only known Frost for two days. How could he know how I felt about him? We had only had one lunch date. Obviously he liked my younger, more popular sister better than me. I had been carried away, that's all. I would give up the whole idea and go back to studying computers. No more Frost for me.

When Janie came home, I tried hard to be cool. "Did you have a good time?"

"Yeah, Frost is a nice guy, Margaret. Alex Pedley and Carol Verson went, too. We're all going to have a beach party on Friday. Sounds like fun, huh?" Janie's voice got very musical when she was excited.

"Sounds great." How was I going to stand a whole evening with Frost as Janie's boyfriend?

"I'll call all the kids tomorrow from work. You tell anyone you see," Janie went on. "Mom said she'd get the bonfire permit."

I pretended to be asleep. My head was shouting at Janie for taking my boyfriend, but the room was quiet. Soon Janie's regular breathing told me she was asleep.

The next morning I drove Janie to work and headed toward the mainland to work on my computer. I had to get away. My stomach was less jumpy when I left the island. I felt free of all the embarrassing boy problems I'd gotten myself into. Give me a computer any day. They're much easier than people.

Later when I felt more relaxed, I went to the beach with my notebook. I was praying I wouldn't see Frost, but suddenly I heard his voice.

"Hi, we missed you yesterday," he said.

"I forgot I had to work. Janie and I alternate days at the store."

"Yes, she told me. Do you want to go for a walk?"

He startled me. "I don't think I should. I . . . I stepped on a sandspur, and my foot is sore."

"Okay, we'll sit here. What are you writing?"

"Nothing. It's just a habit." It was pure torture, trying to act as if nothing had happened.

"Did Janie tell you about the beach party?"

"Yes, it sounds great." I couldn't look at him.

"Good. I think so, too."

A small power boat skimmed across the Gulf, the motor whining in protest at its speed.

"I'd love to have a boat like that," Frost

said, longingly, as it sailed out of sight.

"A lot of my friends have boats." I tried to make conversation.

"My mom was in a boating accident when she was little," Frost said. "She's afraid of boats now. She won't let me have one, no matter how much Dad and I try to convince her."

I wondered if he confided in Janie, too.

*　*　*　*　*

Friday, the day of the beach party, dawned clear and hot. I had walked the beach early, looking for a rain cloud that might cancel the party. When I got back to the house, Janie was in the kitchen with Mom going over the list of groceries. I didn't quite make it to my room.

"Margaret, will you go over to the plaza to get the ice? Mr. Carlson promised us his coolers again," Janie said.

"I guess so. What time?" I mumbled.

"Any time after five. And will you go to the bakery to pick up the sandwich rolls?" Janie added.

"And just what are you going to be doing, taking care of all the people while I do the shopping?"

"Margaret," Mom said. "Janie and I will buy everything else."

"Yes, I know. I know." I went to my room to avoid their wounded looks.

Frost came over while Janie and Mom were at the grocery. He knocked at the back door.

"Hi," I said. "Janie's not here."

"But you are here." He grinned at me. "Want to go for a walk?"

"I have to get ready for the party." I gathered the breakfast dishes.

"Please, Margaret, go for a walk with me," he said. "I want to talk to you."

Frost took my hand as we walked. I liked the feel of my hand in his. But his touch just made me feel more miserable. If only I didn't like him so much.

"Are you mad at me for going to the movies with Janie?" he said in a rush, running his fingers through his hair.

"No, of course not," I protested.

"Good. Janie suggested that we go, you know."

"Janie likes to organize outings," I said.

"I'm looking forward to the beach party," he said.

"So am I." I lied.

* * * * *

I had made twenty trips down to the beach with the food for the party and the emergency buckets in case of fire. I was feeling sticky and uncomfortable. Since Janie was giving the orders, she looked cool and sparkling as usual. The kids had started to arrive, and the radios were blaring before Frost got there. I was still confused about Janie and Frost and me. Did he like her or me? Either way seemed hopeless. Janie seemed to be in love with him, too. She went out to meet him all smiles and introduced him around to all the kids.

Frost came over to me. I was cooking hot dogs. "Hi, Margaret, need any help?"

"No, you go ahead and talk to Janie," I snapped.

"All right, I will," he said and left.

Tears splashed down my cheeks, but I angrily wiped them away. I would not cry.

After we ate, everyone danced to the radio. Howie Jordan kept asking me to dance. Frost danced with Janie and some of the other girls, but not with me. Nancy held up the limbo bar and started a contest to see who could go under it. Frost was terrific at it. Even after everyone else had failed at the lowered bar, Janie kept encouraging Frost.

"Come on, Frost. You can do it." Janie clapped her hands.

"What will you give me if I do, Janie?" He grinned at her.

"Another hot dog." Janie giggled.

"How about a kiss?" Frost said.

Janie giggled louder. "Okay, a kiss."

Of course, Frost slid under the bar. And of course, Janie kissed him right on the lips.

I jumped up and ran down the beach. The cool breeze felt good on my hot face. The sound of the waves lapping at the shore was a welcome change from the blaring radios. I heard someone behind me. When I turned around, there was Frost.

"What's the matter, Margaret? Why are you so edgy?"

"I'm not edgy."

"You push Janie on me, and then you get mad when I'm nice to her." He sounded frustrated.

"I'm not pushing anybody on anybody," I said.

"Are you playing hard to get, Margaret? Because if you are, I'm getting tired of the game."

"Hard to get? Me? I thought you liked Janie. She's always the popular one. I'm the one . . . " I stopped. I was dangerously close to crying again.

"I spent the day with you because I wanted to. Have I spent the day with Janie yet?" His voice was soothing now. He put his arm around me.

"No, but . . . " I wanted to move away from

him, but I didn't.

"Maybe I like you, Margaret."

"I hadn't thought of that." I swallowed the lump in my throat and grinned at him. He lifted my face close to his, and he kissed me. I hadn't ever been kissed with feeling, and I liked it. I liked it so much, I kissed him back. It was such a nice warm, happy feeling. The next thing I did was laugh. Frost must have felt the same way. He laughed, too.

"I've been trying to figure you out for days," I said.

"I could say the same about you," he said. The next natural thing to do was go swimming. So we did. Everybody saw us. Soon the whole party was swimming and ducking each other and laughing.

Afterward Frost helped us carry the food up to the house. Janie was more quiet than usual. Frost and I were laughing at every word we said as if it were a big joke. Later when he kissed me good night, I could see every star in the sky. Here I thought it was going to be an awful party, and it turned out to be a night I'd always remember.

Four

FROST usually showed up on my days off. I always looked forward to seeing him. With Frost I was never sure what was going to happen.

It was his idea to drive to the other end of the island where the most luxurious condos were.

"Only members are admitted there," I said.

"Maybe they'll let us in." Frost grinned. "We won't know until we get there, will we?"

When we drove up to the gate, a red wooden arm blocked the entrance to the Sand Dunes Condominium Resort. The security guard came out of his little building and looked over the top of his glasses at Frost and me. His name tag read, "Gus."

"What do you kids want?" he rasped.

"My father is A.L. Duvall from Orlando. He's in condo conversions, and he sent me out to look over your grounds." Frost handed him his father's business card.

Gus frowned at the card. "Just a minute." He shuffled back inside and picked up the phone.

Frost looked at me and I supressed a giggle. Gus came back out. "I'm sorry, Mr. Duvall. I can't admit anyone without clearance from the office. Tell your father to call, and we'll arrange a visit."

Frost's ears were turning red. "I understand."

We drove back through the trees on the winding road. A small rain cloud had formed off the southern horizon.

"We should have dressed up," Frost exclaimed.

"What?"

"It's our shorts. We look like kids."

"Well, what do you think we are, Zelda and Scott Fitzgerald?" I had written a report on Fitzgerald and *The Great Gatsby* last year in English. I wondered if that would impress Frost.

"I'll tell you what. You dress up like Zelda on Wednesday, and we'll have lunch at the Sand Dunes."

"Do you really think it'll work?"

"I can't wait to see the look on Gus's face." He grinned.

* * * * *

I spent Wednesday morning getting ready. I couldn't decide what to wear. All my clothes made me look too young. My heart was pounding as if we were planning to rob a bank.

"Janie, Frost is taking me to a fancy place for lunch. What should I wear?" I asked.

"Your lavender dress," Janie said.

"My lavender dress has ruffles. I want to look older."

"Then wear your white skirt with the slit in it and my red tank top."

"No, that's too sexy. I want to look like Zelda Fitzgerald."

"I don't know her, but how about my beige and red Hawaiian shirt over the tank top?"

"Perfect. May I wear your white sandals, too?"

"Sure. This must be some lunch." She looked a tiny bit envious, I thought.

"Thanks, Janie."

"So long, I'm late for work," Janie called on her way out.

After she left, I made up my face with everything I could find in her makeup drawer. I tried all my sultry model looks in the mirror, and then I laughed out loud. It wasn't really me, but it was fun pretending.

I sneaked out the back door. I didn't want Mom to see my face. She would have asked me if I were going to a costume party. That's

27

one of her standard lines when Janie wears too much makeup to school.

The hot sun was driving me crazy. My face felt as if it were painted stiff. Fortunately Frost was on time.

"You look terrific," he said as he opened the car door for me.

"You look pretty neat yourself." He wore white pants and a navy blazer with a red shirt open at the neck.

When we pulled up at the gate, Gus peered at us closely trying to hide his surprise at our appearance. Frost and I didn't dare look at each other.

"Yes, Mr. Duvall, you're expected," Gus said.

The dining room was pretty dark so it took us awhile to adjust our eyes. I just about walked into a potted fern. The waiter showed us to our seats by the window overlooking the same beach we saw every day. Through the windows the beach looked richer. I was enchanted with Frost. He was doing such a thorough job of trying to look older he almost convinced me.

"Phew. Some place," I whispered.

"I told you I'd get in, didn't I?" Frost whispered back. I didn't know why we were being so quiet, because there weren't over five other people in the whole place.

When I read the menu, I began to worry about prices again. They didn't have hot dogs.

"How can you tell what to order?" Frost whispered.

"The menu's in French," I said.

"Can you translate?"

"I'll try. I knew a little French from school." I figured out the main categories like fish and meat, but from there on we had to guess.

We ordered two fish dishes. Mine turned out to be a shrimp salad big enough for six people. Frost's was broiled trout almondine. The waiters hovered about five feet behind us.

"If I yell 'fire,' do you think they would leave us alone?" Frost whispered.

"Don't make me laugh," I said.

"Why? If you laugh, will your makeup crack?"

Suddenly everything seemed hilarious. I fought to keep a straight face. It was like trying not to laugh in church.

"It's all right, Margaret, you're allowed two giggles before they throw you out of here."

I choked on a mouthful of shrimp. I gave Frost a dirty look. "No more," I said. "I can't eat and giggle, too."

We ate silently. I dared not look at Frost. I was a time bomb of giggles about to go off.

"I don't think I can eat any more," Frost said.

"I know I can't." There was a slight dent in my mountain of shrimp.

Frost motioned to the waiter. He took the plates away and brought the check. He seemed annoyed that we ate so little. I found that funny. Of course, I found everything funny. When we finally got to the car, I laughed all the way home.

"What's the matter?" Frost asked.

"I don't know. My side aches. I think being so dignified got to me."

"Well you have to admit, it was an experience," he said.

"Zelda and Fitzgerald never had a better time."

*   *   *   *   *

That night Janie asked me if I wanted to double date to the movies with Allen and her. I didn't answer at first. I was still touchy about Janie and Frost being together. I remembered the nightmare of Frost going to the movies with Janie. Then there was the beach party. The farther Frost stayed away from Janie, the better I liked it. But in her usual organized way, Janie kept after me until I called Frost and asked what he wanted to do. Of course he said it was up to me. So I had to say yes. Sometimes I wonder how I get myself into such messes. I knew from the start it was a mistake.

First of all, Janie was in one of her personality plus moods. No boy could have resisted her. She wore white jeans and a red ruffled blouse that exposed her tanned shoulders. Both Allen and Frost stared at her immediately. Her eyes cast some hypnotic spell over them. Even I was mesmerized.

Of course, she maneuvered it so she sat between Allen and Frost at the theater. All the way through the movie, she whispered to them. I couldn't hear a word she said, but it seemed like she talked to Frost more than Allen. I was furious.

"What shall we do now?" Frost asked, when the movie was over.

"What do you want to do, Frost?" Janie's voice was musical.

"We could go for a walk on the beach," Allen mumbled.

I felt as sorry for Allen as I did myself. Janie took him for granted because he was so good-natured.

"How about a hot fudge sundae?" Frost asked.

Everyone agreed it was a good idea. I didn't want to prolong the torture, so I ate my sundae as fast as I could. Finally we finished, and Allen said he had to get home. When we pulled into his driveway, he didn't waste any time getting out of the car.

At our house I thought Janie would never go inside. She wanted to see all the constellations in the sky. She asked Frost to help her hunt for them. I was so mad I didn't think I would ever speak to her again. Finally she said good night.

"I don't know what happened to her tonight," I said. We sat on the porch steps looking at the stars.

"She's just a very outgoing girl," Frost said.

"You can say that again."

"Janie thrives on other people's attention." Frost took my hand.

"Is that what you call it?"

"You sound bitter, Margaret."

"Janie's such a flirt. I felt sorry for Allen."

"Your problem is the more Janie flirts, the more you pout."

"How is that a problem?"

"Then you don't have any fun."

"How could I have fun while Janie is flirting with my date." I almost said boyfriend, but I stopped myself.

"If you talked more, she might tone down a little."

"I doubt it."

"You'll never know until you try." He smiled in the dark. "Besides I might enjoy your flirting more than Janie's."

"Hmmm . . ." Maybe he's right, I thought.

Frost squeezed my hand. We said good night after a few minutes. It was amazing how easily Frost could talk me out of being mad.

Five

I wanted a new outfit to wear to Freddie's annual Fourth of July dance. The first thing I thought of was hunting shells on Captiva. Mom always paid us wholesale prices for rare shells. I asked Frost to go with me.

"Six o'clock?" he said. "Only those little birds get up that early. What are their names, those ones that run around in the sand?"

"Sandpipers. But the best shelling is early in the morning."

"I'll pick you up at seven-thirty. No earlier," he said.

* * * * *

Here I was, standing in front of my house at seven-thirty and no Frost. The morning was cloudy so the Gulf looked gray and iridescent. The eastern sky was streaked with red and rain clouds. But usually the sun burned the clouds off by noon. The real rain always came later in the afternoon.

Frost grinned as he drove up. "Got here as fast as I could."

"What time did you get up?" I teased.

"Five minutes ago." He looked at his watch.

I laughed. "I'd say you're pretty speedy."

"My mother heard that the best shelling is on Sanibel," Frost said. "Why are we going to Captiva?"

"Sanibel is famous for its shelling, but some rare shells hit Captiva, too. Nobody goes there to look, so we might get lucky," I explained.

The drive was long but pleasant under the cover of the live oak trees. We left the car at a central point. This way we could explore the coast on both sides and never be far from our cooler of food and drinks. I had brought shovels and pails to carry our loot. Frost paced the beach looking for shells.

"No, not that way," I called to him.

"What's the problem? I haven't seen any shells yet," he said.

"Do it like this." I strolled slowly through the shallow water. When my foot felt a smooth object, I located the shell. I pulled up an olive shell triumphantly.

"You have talented feet," Frost said, grinning.

He tried to copy me. At first he shuffled too much and made the water cloudy. After awhile he slowed down and got better results.

"Hey, I found one," Frost said.

"Good, what is it?" I called.

He pulled it up and wiped it off. "I don't know."

"It's a king's crown. And it's in good condition, too. It's the best find so far," I congratulated him.

"See, I catch on quick."

"Let's stop for lunch and celebrate," I suggested.

"That's the best idea you've had all day."

We trudged back to the car. I traded our buckets for the basket lunch I had packed for us. Frost objected to washing his hands in salt water, but he did it anyway. We chose a small, grassy knoll overlooking the gulf. It was shaded by the lush trees that were everywhere on Captiva.

"I brought ham and Swiss on rye and peanut butter and jelly," I said.

"Ham and cheese, please," Frost said.

We ate mostly in silence. I was trying to add up the worth of our find so far. Most of the shells were common and not worth much except for the king's crown. Since it was in such good shape, it might bring seventy-five cents. It wasn't enough for a new outfit for the dance. I visualized the red shorts and the red and white striped shirt I had picked out at

Meribee's, the island sportswear shop.

"What are you so serious about?" Frost asked.

"I was thinking about how much money we're going to make," I said.

"Let's forget the whole thing and go swimming." He grabbed my hand.

"I can't. I need the money."

"I'll give you the money. It's no problem. Breaking my back and straining my eyes to see tiny shells is a problem."

"You said you wanted to come." I jumped up. "Besides, my mom needs the shells for her shop. And I don't want you to give me any money."

"Don't get excited. I'm sorry," Frost said and squeezed my arm. I did want to come."

He said it so sweetly. It was impossible to be upset with Frost. I smiled at him and went back for my pail.

We worked apart for a while, but we didn't come up with anything unusual. When the sun began to shine in my eyes, I knew it was time to go home. But as I peered across the island, something caught my eye. Piles of shells had been pocketed behind the trees by the high tide. I wandered back through the trees, not thinking of anything but the dollar signs that were dancing in my eyes.

"Frost, look what I found." I held up a

fourteen inch conch.

"That's a beaut," he called.

I placed it carefully in my pail and kept digging. Some other large shells were half buried in the soft sand and partially covered by grass and undergrowth. I worked quickly. I uncovered three conchs, two king's crowns and several olives. My pail was full, and I stood up to stretch my cramped back. Then I saw them. I guess I felt the pain at the same time.

"Ouch," I yelled. I ran for the water. "Red ants," I yelled louder. "Ooh, those horrible red ants." I stamped up and down in the water too angry to cry. "How could I have been so stupid not to feel them biting me?"

"Are you all right?" Frost peered at me. "Can I do anything?"

I sat down in the water and rubbed my feet. The bites covered each foot and were swelling into red welts.

"How could I be so stupid?" I shrieked again, ignoring him.

"Let's see." Frost grabbed my feet. "Looks bad all right. Maybe we'll have to amputate at the knee."

"A lot you know about it," I snarled. "I'm allergic to red ants. My feet swell way up and I can't walk for days." The tears streamed down my face.

"Well, it won't do any good to sit in the Gulf

and cry about it," Frost said. He didn't understand.

I leaned on Frost's arm and hobbled to the car. He soaked my beach towel in salt water and wrapped my feet for the ride home. I was so furious, I could do nothing but sit there and feel my feet grow hotter.

It began to drizzle just enough that Frost had to turn the windshield wipers on and off. By the time we got home, my feet felt like they had needles in the bottom when I tried to stand. Frost picked me up and carried me to the house.

"What's wrong? Are you sick?" Janie met us at the door.

"She got bitten by red ants," Frost said. He acted like I was unconscious or something.

"Oh, dear. Put her on the couch," Janie said. "I'll get the soaking solution Dr. Meyer gave us."

Frost went out to get the pails and the cooler. I lay there, angry and hurting. My head felt swollen, too.

"Well, I hope you feel better," Frost said. "I'll see you." He winked at me.

"Thanks for bringing her home," Janie said, as she walked him to the door. She acted like I was a sick puppy or something.

When I opened my eyes, it was dark. Janie was watching TV. My feet were in a pan of tepid water. I felt cold, but my feet were hot. I sloshed my feet around to see how swollen they were.

"How are you feeling?" Janie asked.

"Terrible. What time is it?"

"Ten o'clock. Are you hungry? You fell asleep before I could give you the antihistamine," she said.

"Where are Mom and Dad?" I took the pill she gave me.

"They went to the Thompson's for dinner. They'll be here soon."

"I'm not hungry. I'm just mad." Fresh tears stung my eyes. "Now that I found enough shells to buy a new outfit at Meribee's, I won't be able to go to the dance. My feet will be too swollen."

"Oh, Margaret, maybe the swelling will go down by then. It's two days off."

"You know it won't. It took four days before I could walk the last time. I have more bites now. I was so stupid not to notice those terrible ants."

"Why don't you eat something. You'll feel better."

"I'm not hungry."

"Did Frost get bitten, too?"

"No, why?"

"I just wondered if he would be going to the dance."

"Oh, great. Just take my boyfriend, you little vulture." I started to cry.

"Margaret, don't be so melodramatic." Janie chuckled.

Her laughing made me cry harder. "You just want him because he's my boyfriend, that's all."

Mom and Dad came home. "What happened? Are you all right?"

"She got bitten by ants," Janie said. "And she's all hyper."

"I've got a lot to be hyper about, Janie," I yelled.

"My goodness, shouting isn't going to help," Mom said. She felt my forehead.

"Would you like something to eat, a bowl of soup maybe?"

I tried to control my anger. "Yeah, anything but chicken noodle." I stared at the TV, not really seeing it.

"Janie, I think the swelling is going down now. Maybe I will be able to go to Freddie's on the Fourth," I said, trying to sound convincing.

"You really think so? Well, sure you will. But don't worry. If you can't, Allen and I will take care of Frost for you."

"Yeah, sure." I couldn't fight anymore.

Mom came in with the soup. "Chicken noodle was the only kind I had, dear. Try to eat a little."

Six

IT was one of those days with two kinds of weather. Either rain drizzled out of gray clouds or poured out of black clouds. Inside the house it was gloomy all day, too. The ant bites stuck up like white pimples against my red feet. Since I could hardly move my toes or ankles, walking was difficult and painful. Dancing was impossible.

I wanted so badly to go to the dance at Freddie's boardwalk and show Frost off to my friends. Since Nancy had spred the word, everybody wanted to meet him. But I had to stay home with swollen feet while my cute, popular sister, who always had lots of boyfriends, took my boyfriend to the dance.

My mind kept thinking of all the ways Frost could fall in love with Janie. I saw them dancing together, smiling at each other, talking intimately, even kissing. It was pure torture.

The TV predicted rain for the Fourth. That was one glimmer of hope in my gloomy future.

Rain would keep a lot of people home. If they had to hold the dance inside, only half as many kids would see Frost with Janie.

"Where's Janie?" I asked. She hadn't come home with Mom. Maybe she had developed measles or had ten zits on her nose or had broken both legs.

"She had some errands to do," Mom said.

Just then the door opened. Janie walked in looking fresh and beautiful. She smiled at me. "How are you feeling, Margaret?"

I hated her so much. How could she be so smug and sure of herself? Why couldn't she have at least one zit or look a little tired?

"Here." She held out a paper bag from Meribee's. "I didn't have time to wrap it."

"What is it?"

"It's a present, silly. Open it."

I stared at her. A person as awful as Janie wouldn't be giving me a present.

"Margaret, is your brain swollen, too?"

"Thank you," I said, sarcastically. I opened the bag and took out something wrapped in tissue paper. It was the red cotton shorts I had wanted for the dance. I was speechless.

"I cleaned your shells and took them to Mom's shop. There was just enough money for the shorts. I couldn't afford the shirt. When you're feeling better, you can wear my white shirt with them."

"All that work. Oh, Janie." I hugged her and tears welled up in my eyes. I was crying because she was being so nice when I hated her so. I was also crying because now I had the red shorts, and I still couldn't go to the dance.

"Hey, I got them to cheer you up," Janie said.

"I know, I know," I said, wiping away my tears.

The Fourth of July dawned bright and sunny. I scanned the sky in every direction, but there were no rain clouds. I hadn't seen Frost since the horrible trip to Captiva. Janie said he had called after I went to bed last night. Of course, she talked to him. When he showed up at our back door, I wasn't surprised.

"Hello, Miss Queen of the Swollen Feet. How is your health today?" Frost bowed low before me and made a face at my ugly feet.

I giggled. "At least you're not telling me there will be other dances."

"May there never be another dance as long as you live, milady, at which you are the Queen of the Swollen Feet." He used an official-sounding voice.

"Here, here," I said. "Janie promises to take good care of you tonight."

"One cannot come to Sanibel without attending the infamous Fourth of July dance at Freddie's," Frost observed.

"That's true. I wish I could go."

"Maybe you won't miss much," he said. "I'm not big on dances anyway."

"You're not?"

"Who knows, you might have had a rotten time with me."

"You're just trying to cheer me up. I've never had a rotten time with you," I said.

"Thank you for the compliment." He bowed again, but this time he kissed me briefly instead of looking at my feet.

Janie came in to say good-bye. She looked so pretty I wanted to cry all over again. She wore pale pink shorts and a pastel striped shirt of pink and blue. I told her to have a good time at the dance, but my mind was saying just the opposite.

After she left, I had a mild attack of the guilts. How could I hate Janie when she cleaned my shells and bought me the shorts? And Frost . . . I thought he wanted to go with Janie, and he said he didn't even like dances. I sloshed my feet around in the water. I wished I could do something to avoid thinking so much. I wished I had the computer in front of me. Then I could lose myself for a few hours and forget about the stupid dance. I had to settle for watching reruns on TV.

It seemed like hours later when Janie

tiptoed across our darkened room.

"Did you have a good time?" I whispered.

"Oh, Margaret, it was divine. You don't know how much fun it is to have two dates," Janie gushed.

"No, I don't." I was mad already.

"First, I had to explain to everyone about your feet and who Frost was. It was such a good story that it got everybody in a laughing mood. You know what I mean?"

"I certainly do."

"Then Allen and Frost were competing for how attentive they could be. It was so much fun."

"You're too much, Janie."

"I'm so tired. I think I danced every dance. Frost is such a fantastic dancer. I bet my feet hurt as much as yours do tonight." She whirled around the room.

"Frost is a good dancer?"

"He's the best dancer I've ever danced with. He looked so dreamy with his dark hair and his pale pink shirt. We made a really cute couple on the dance floor. Everyone was staring at us."

I couldn't trust myself to talk at this point.

"Allen wore a light blue shirt. He looked dreamy, too. It was so much fun knowing every person in the whole place was watching me."

"Oh, Janie, shut up will you?" I shouted.

"Margaret, you're always in a bad mood, you know that?" Janie stomped off to the bathroom.

Frost lied to me! I thought. He said he didn't like dances, and then he turns out to be the best dancer. What else had he lied to me about? He could be dating Janie on alternate days for all I knew.

My anger swept over me in waves. Janie had gotten my sympathy, too. She bought me the shorts to make me think she was nice, but she was rotten. I would never trust either of them again. But I won't give up Frost without a fight, I thought. I couldn't. It would hurt too much.

Seven

I was sitting on the back porch the next afternoon when Frost stopped by.

"How was the dance?" I asked him.

"I had a better time than I expected," he said.

"Janie was very impressed with your dancing."

"It seemed to be the thing to do." Frost laughed weakly.

"You're not as funny as you were yesterday," I said.

He gave me a strange look. Anger was stealing over me, tensing my muscles. I wanted to shout at him for having such a good time and for lying to me.

I took a deep breath. "The swelling has gone down some. See?" I held up one foot.

"I'm glad. We'll be looking for shells again soon. Only we'll watch out for ants next time."

"Janie cleaned all the shells we found and got me some red shorts with the money," I said.

"Janie's quite a girl," Frost said.

What did he mean by that? How I hated hidden meanings. Life was so much easier before Frost came along. I tried to think of what Janie would do. I decided to try to be nice no matter how I felt inside.

"How did your windsurfing lesson go today?" I asked in my most cheerful voice.

"I stayed up on the board longer today than I ever have."

"That's marvelous," I said gaily.

"Are you feet feeling better now?" he said.

"They're fine, thank you."

Frost stopped suddenly. "Margaret, what's with you?"

"What do you mean?"

"Why are you acting so formal?"

"I'm not. It must be your imagination."

"Are you mad at me for dancing with Janie at the dance? Well, what did you expect me to do? Sit in the corner?"

"Why would I be mad at you? No, I'm not mad." I turned away from him.

After awhile he said, "I guess I'd better go."

Frost walked away. He looked grim and angry. I felt bad. Why hadn't I told him how hurt I was?

I turned to go inside. The screen door banged behind me. I only got as far as the kitchen. Janie was standing in the doorway, her hands on her hips.

"Why were you so mean to Frost?" she asked.

"Don't start on me. I'm not in the mood for it," I snarled.

"What's going on?" Janie persisted.

"Leave me alone. Nothing is going on." I slipped past her and started down the hall.

"All right. I guess I'll have to tell Mom you're being rotten to everyone."

I hesitated. "I'm mad at you for having so much fun with Frost at the Fourth of July dance."

"For heaven's sake, what did you want me to do, ignore him?"

There's more to it than that. He told me he didn't like to dance. Then he danced almost every dance with you," I said.

The tears came gushing down. When was I going to be old enough to turn off the waterworks?

"Margaret, I asked him to dance. He was being polite."

"Sounds like he enjoyed himself."

"He still likes you better than me. He was polite to me, nothing more."

"Yeah, I bet."

"It's the truth, Margaret. Why don't you believe me?"

I wanted to say more. I wanted to tell her

how popular I thought she was and how unpopular I was. I couldn't bring myself to say it, because I was the older sister. I was supposed to know more than Janie. Well, I didn't.

"I don't want to talk anymore. I'm going to bed," I said.

"What else is bothering you? I'd like to settle this," Janie said.

"That's all. Good night."

"First I get Allen mad at me for being nice to Frost, and now you're mad at me. No matter what I try to do, I can't win," Janie said. "Good night."

Eight

THE telephone woke me up. It was Mr. Langley, my computer instructor. "Margaret, how are you? We have double enrollment for the beginning two-week course. How would you like to help me out as an assistant instructor? The job pays two hundred dollars."

"Yes, I'd like to," I said without thinking. Two hundred dollars sounded like a lot for my college fund.

"Fine. See you Monday at nine o'clock." He hung up.

"Who was that?" Mom asked.

As I told her about Mr. Langley's offer, I realized I wouldn't see Frost for two weeks. Janie would be here to entertain him. How could I have been so stupid to say yes?

I made myself a gigantic bowl of cereal. In between shouts on TV, I heard a faint knock at the door. Mom answered it.

"It's Bill Creamer, Margaret," she called.

"Oh, no!" I had slept in a T-shirt and

underwear. I raced to my room and pulled on my shorts before Bill saw me. I swiped at my tangled hair with my brush.

"Bill, what are you doing out so early?" I asked.

"Sorry to get you up." Bill grinned. "Mr. Langley hired me, too. I came over to see if I could bum a ride to school with you."

"Yeah, he just called. Sure, you can ride with me."

"I'll pay the toll," Bill declared.

I laughed. He was such a perfectionist about some things. "Do you want to walk on the beach?" Mom was taking in every word.

"I'm free until Monday." Bill shrugged.

I changed into my suit and we left. The cloudless sky was pale blue this morning and the ocean, a darker blue. Quiet waves lapped at the shore. Being with Bill was fun. I hadn't realized how much I missed him. Seeing him was like looking at school yearbooks and recalling all the good times.

"How's your summer going so far?" Bill asked.

"Interesting," I said. "I have a boyfriend. Oops, now what did I go and say that for?" I bonged myself on the forehead.

Bill laughed. "You're a riot, Margaret. I always laugh when I'm with you."

"You do? I wonder what my secret is?

Nobody else finds me funny lately."

"That's hard to believe. So who's the boyfriend and why doesn't he think you are funny?"

We sat down on the beach. I found myself pouring out the whole story of Frost and Janie and me. I never planned a truth session, but Bill seemed to be a good listener. Having someone to talk to felt almost as good as swimming in the early morning when the cool salt water still shocked me.

"Now, I've told Mr. Langley I will help with the course, but I'm afraid to leave Frost in Janie's clutches," I finished.

"Sounds complicated," Bill agreed.

"I didn't realize how complicated relationships could be," I said.

"I saw a movie once where two girls were fighting over the same guy," Bill said. "The guy got tired of the two girls bickering over him so he went off and started dating a third girl. The first two girls were both out of luck," Bill said.

"Do you think Janie and I are fighting over Frost?"

"You said the relationship was getting complicated."

I thought about it for a minute. Frost could get tired of trying to please us both.

"Bill, I'm glad you came over. I'll do the

computer course," I said. "Want to swim?"

We got up and ran into the Gulf. Bill was the opposite of Frost. He had dark hair, but he was thinner and seemed younger. His hair hung down straight from a severe part, making him look much more serious and bookish than he really was.

When we returned to the house, Mom had tuna sandwiches waiting for us. I invited Bill to stay for lunch. We rinsed off under the outdoor shower and ate at the picnic table in our backyard.

"Did you know Mr. Langley is getting married in August?" Bill asked.

"You're kidding. Who is he marrying?"

"Miss Peterson."

"Irene Peterson, the gym teacher?" I laughed.

"What's so funny?" I recognized Frost's voice.

"Hi, Frost. This is Bill Creamer. He's a friend from school." I smiled at Bill. "Bill, this is Frost Duvall."

"Glad to meet you," Bill said.

"Hi." Frost shook Bill's hand.

"Would you like some lunch?" Having two boys looking at me was a pleasant experience.

"No, I just ate," Frost said.

Bill and I resumed our lunch, but it seemed strange with Frost sitting there.

"We were talking about Mr. Langley and Miss Peterson," I explained. "They're getting married."

"You'd have to know them," Bill said. "The odd couple?"

Frost grinned, expecting more.

Mom came out with a plate of brownies. "Thanks, Mom. Those look good," I said, relieved that she had interrupted us.

Mom smiled knowingly and went back in. Frost took a brownie. We munched silently.

"Bill and I are going to help teach a beginning computer class next week," I said.

"That's great for you, Margaret. I know how you love computers," Frost said, glancing at Bill.

"I'm looking forward to it," I said.

Finally Bill said he had to get home. "Thanks for lunch. I'll see you Monday." He retrieved his bicycle from the side of the house and took off. He grinned and waved when he reached the end of the driveway.

I waved back. I was disappointed he left even though things had been a little strained between Frost and him. Maybe that's how Frost felt when he was with Janie and me.

"Why so thoughtful?" Frost asked.

"No reason," I said. "Bill will be riding with me to school next week."

"Have you ever dated Bill?"

"Once. But we're just good friends," I said, smiling.

Frost grinned back. "Want to go swimming?"

"Sure." We raced down to the water.

"Margaret, the computer kid," Frost said, when he came up for air.

"That's me," I gasped.

He teased me all afternoon, and I enjoyed it. I wondered what put me in such a good mood, Frost or the thought of working on the computer for two weeks.

* * * * *

When I picked Bill up Monday morning, he was jovial. "So how's the boyfriend? How'd he get a name like Frost?"

"He was named after his grandfather's company. You know, Frost Cooling Systems, Inc.?"

"No kidding? I'm glad my dad didn't name me after his store. How'd you like to be named Tru-Value?"

We laughed as we approached the toll booth. Bill handed over the three dollars.

The day went quickly. Teaching beginners was easy, because they knew nothing at all about computers. Usually unscrambling their mistakes was easy, too.

"I'd bet you're thinking about your

boyfriend instead of the computer," Bill guessed on the way home.

"You'd bet right," I said with a smile.

"He sure is lucky," Bill said.

"He changed his windsurfing class from afternoon to morning so he could see me when I got home," I said.

"It must be true love," Bill sang out.

I smiled again. The idea warmed me to my toes, but I couldn't get carried away. I remembered Janie and the dance at Freddie's.

I dropped Bill off and headed for home. I could see Frost's car a block away. In spite of my warnings to myself, coming home and finding Frost there was like a special celebration. I hoped he was there to see me and not Janie.

"Hi," Frost said, and opened the car door for me. "I missed you."

He always said the right things. "I missed you, too," I said.

Janie and Allen came strolling out the door. "All right, you two . . ." Janie giggled.

They were arm in arm. All my little brain cells tingled when I saw them. The four of us walked on the beach for a while.

"Allen, why are you walking so funny?" I asked.

"Football practice started today," Allen said. "Every muscle in my body hurts."

"You poor thing," Janie said, reaching up to rub his back.

"The cool water feels good," Allen said, wading up to his knees in the waves.

"The water feels warm to me," Frost said.

"It seems cool compared to how hot I was today," Allen said. "How did the computer class go, Margaret?"

"Great," I said. "It's so much fun that the day rushes by."

"Wish I could say that about football practice," Allen groaned.

"Think how glad you'll be this fall when you cream all those other teams," Janie said.

"Yeah. And you'll be cheering me on," Allen said. "When do you go to cheerleading camp?"

Janie's smile faded. "In two weeks, I think."

"Did you know Janie is head cheerleader of Ft. Myer's High?" Allen asked Frost.

"How do you do, Head Cheerleader?" Frost bowed.

Janie smiled. Mom called us for dinner, so we had to go in. It seemed like such a short time to spend with Frost when I was used to spending the whole day with him. I stored away in my memory bank every word he said and every curve of his smile.

Each morning I was glad to see Bill, and in the evenings I looked forward to being with Frost. I was different with each of them, and that was all right, I thought. I was Margaret, the computer whiz kid. I had a friend named Bill who made me laugh. I also had a friend named Frost who made me feel special. And I had a sister named Janie who was popular with boys. But then I was beginning to think I was popular, too. Well . . . maybe just a little.

Nine

AS I plodded up from the beach, I could hear Janie arguing with Mom. Janie had been crabby lately. She frowned more than she smiled, and that was unusual for her.

"I'm sorry," Janie whined.

" 'I'm sorry' doesn't get me to the store on time. Hurry up," Mom said.

I hesitated at the door but went in anyway. Janie had tears in her eyes. She was in front of the mirror tying her hair ribbon. Mom was tight-lipped and silent.

* * * * *

When I came home in the afternoon, I was hit with the same gloom I had felt that morning. Janie was watching the soaps on TV.

"What's up, Janie? Is anything wrong?" I asked.

"Cheerleading camp starts next week," she said. "I'm only the head cheerleader, and Mom says we have no money for camp."

"Can't you take it out of your college fund?"

"Mom won't let me. She says college is more important than cheerleading."

Mom had dropped out of college to marry Dad. Ever since then she had been determined to educate Janie and me.

"I didn't realize money was so scarce," I said.

"Dad hasn't had a good summer in real estate. And the store is barely paying its bills." Janie sounded bitter.

"How much do you need?"

"Two hundred dollars."

"You can have my money from the computer class," I said.

"Oh, no, Margaret, that's for your college fund." Janie shook her head. "Besides Mom wouldn't let you do that any more than she'd let me take it out of my bank account."

"You're probably right," I said. "But don't worry. We'll get the money somehow."

Frost stopped by and we went for a walk on the beach. He told me about the boardsail he was buying. It somehow didn't seem fair that he could spend several hundred dollars on a boardsail when our family had to weigh each purchase so carefully.

"When are you going to let me see your computer?" Frost asked.

"I guess you could go to class with me if you want to. You'd have to be very quiet though."

"I'll be a model student. How about Friday?" He grinned.

"Fine."

"I'll drive."

"We have to pick up Bill," I reminded him.

"I was hoping you'd forget."

We watched the sunset turn the sky from flaming orange to muted purple. We said good night reluctantly. Lightning flickered in the east, promising rain.

The tension in the house promised a sure fight. I could tell that as soon as I entered.

Dad was slumped in his chair. Mom was nervously trying to read a book. Janie was staring intently at the TV set. I wished there were something I could say, but I wasn't very good at mediating. Janie was always the one to smooth things over.

"Is anybody hungry? I could make some popcorn." It was a feeble attempt, but at least I tried.

"There's no sense in our sitting here, pretending," Dad began. "Janie is pouting because she wants something we don't have. There's not enough money for cheerleading camp." He got up. "I'm going to bed."

Janie ran to her room sobbing. She yelled terrible things. She went on about Mom and

Dad wanting her to be popular but not giving her money for camp. "How do they expect me to be popular if I'm not a cheerleader?" she shouted.

I was surprised. Did Janie believe her popularity was dependent on cheerleading? I had never seen Janie have any doubts about herself before.

* * * * *

Two days later Dad pulled two hundred-dollar bills out of his pocket. He handed them to Janie at the breakfast table. "I had some money coming from a rental I had forgotten about." His face looked puffy and old when he said it.

"Thanks, Dad." Janie hugged him for a long time. She appeared meek and maybe a little ashamed she had put up a fight. But I knew the fight had come out of her misery, not out of desire to wear my parents down.

The gloom was suddenly lifted. Janie laughed and giggled as before, and everybody smiled. The affect Janie had on people was amazing.

Frost and I drove Janie to Debbie Webber's house, the meeting place of all the cheerleaders. I have never before seen so many giggly, excited girls in one spot.

"Bye, Margaret. Thanks for everything," Janie said a million times.

"Bye. Have a good time," I said.

Frost shook his head when we got back in the car. "What a bunch of noisy females."

"To be a cheerleader, you have to be noisy," I said.

* * * * *

The next day our house seemed like a tomb. There was no Janie to spark our conversations. Dad left early, and Mom and I were locked in our separate worlds. I didn't even bother to get up early to swim. I knew it was going to be an awful day.

First of all, the car wouldn't start. I had to call the service station and have them bring jumper cables. By the time I got to Bill's house, he was frantically pacing the driveway.

"Where have you been? It's nine o'clock already."

"My car wouldn't start," I explained.

"Well, you could have called. I thought you forgot me."

"I wouldn't forget you. We'll have to explain to Mr. Langely, that's all."

"You know how anxious he is to leave every afternoon. Did you see Miss Peterson pick him up yesterday?"

"Yeah. He looked pretty glad to see her."

Bill seemed to relax a bit. "Well, after tomorrow only one more week to go, and then we get our two hundred dollars."

"By the way, Frost is driving us to school tomorrow," I said.

"Why? Are you having your car worked on?"

"No, I invited Frost to see the computer." I paid the toll and took off across the bridge as fast as I could.

"You did what? Margaret, you know that's against the rules." Bill was frantic again. "Watch that car."

"Mr. Langley won't mind. I'll ask him today."

"Oh, sure. You come in late today and then casually ask him to break the rules tomorrow. That'll go over big."

"Okay, so I won't ask him. Don't get excited."

"I think you're making a mistake, that's all."

"I gathered that."

We arrived at 9:30. Mr. Langley's face had a pinched look like something smelled bad. The back of his neck was bright red. When I explained my car failure, he just mumbled and resumed the class.

* * * * *

When I woke up Friday morning, I felt a sense of foreboding. All the time I was getting dressed, I worried about telling Mr. Langley that Frost was coming to class today.

"Well, here it is," I said, when the three of us arrived at the computer room. I walked around the room, flipping on all the terminals at the student desks.

"There's a lot of equipment," Frost said. "How does it work?"

"Suppose you want to add all the even integers between one and one hundred," I said. "Quick, what's the answer?"

Frost shook his head. "Beats me."

I sat down at one of the terminals and typed out the program. Then I typed the command "RUN," and in two seconds I had the answer.

"So that's all there is to it," Frost said.

"It's more complicated than it looks," Bill said.

"Let me show you another of our programs," I said. I punched out the statements and commands. The video screen lighted up. I explained it to Frost.

"Very useful stuff," Frost said.

"Computers are the workers of the future," Bill snapped. "Anybody who doesn't see it has sand in his brain."

"Bill." I glared at him.

Frost grinned. "Margaret sort of likes my

67

sandy brain . . . don't you?" He put his arm around me.

Bill dropped the ream of computer paper he was carrying. It scattered all over the floor, knocking the American flag off its stand. The flagpole smashed across the keyboard of the computer. The crash echoed loudly.

"Oh, no," I said.

Video display flashed, ERROR—ERROR. Frost quit grinning and looked at the screen.

"The program's ruined!" Bill shouted, rushing over to the terminal.

"I can correct it," I said.

I pressed the buttons, but nothing I did eliminated the ERROR sign.

"Now we've done it, Margaret. I told you bringing him was trouble." Bill swung the terminal toward him and frantically tried everything he knew to correct the program.

I grabbed the computer manual and flipped the pages. I couldn't find a clue to help us. "I think we have to cancel the whole program," I said.

"Don't you realize that's a whole week's work?" Bill snapped.

I didn't answer. I was staring at the door. Mr. Langley had just walked in. His face turned purple.

"What's going on here?" he demanded.

"I made an error that I can't seem to

correct," I said in a small voice.

Mr. Langley sat down slowly at the terminal. He pushed several buttons with no luck. The computer was making a strange humming sound. "Exactly how did this happen?"

"I was showing Frost how the program looks," I began. I tried to show Mr. Langley the sequence I had typed out. "Then the flag accidentally fell on the keyboard."

Mr. Langley listened, his hand covering his mouth as if he didn't trust himself to speak. "I see. We'll have to call a repairman." He got up and walked behind the computer. He pulled the plug. The silence was the most awful sound I had ever heard.

"The programs are all lost," Bill croaked.

"Every one of them," Mr. Langley said.

"I'm sorry," I whispered.

"Who are you?" Mr. Langley turned to Frost.

I introduced them. The students were clustered around the door, but seeing the intense red on Mr. Langley's face, no one had ventured inside.

"Be in my office on Monday morning at nine o'clock, both of you." He looked at Bill and me. Then he walked over to the others. "Class is dismissed for today," he said.

No one talked on the way home. Bill had added angry to his frantic look. I felt like a big weight had been placed on my head. It was pounding me into the ground. I couldn't breathe. Not only did I feel responsible for ruining all the students' programs, but also for breaking the machine. Who knows what it would cost to get it fixed?

Raindrops splashed on the windshield when we got to Bill's house. He ran in without saying anything.

"Margaret, I'm sorry about the computer. If I hadn't gone with you, it wouldn't have been broken," Frost said, his voice thick. "I guess Bill was right. I didn't belong there."

"It would have been all right if I had gotten permission," I said without much conviction. I didn't want him to feel responsible.

"Let me know what the instructor says, okay?"

"I will. But it wasn't your fault. It was an accident."

"I was teasing Bill because he was being such a pain," he said. He squeezed my fingers.

"I know. It was a comedy of errors," I said. Frost twisted his mouth into a half smile.

"No pun intended," I said.

Ten

ON Monday morning I picked Bill up right on time. He was waiting in the middle of the road like an anxious hitchhiker.

"Did you hear from Mr. Langley?"

"No," I said.

"I wonder what they will do to us?" Bill asked.

"Maybe we'll be deported," I said. Bill had such a nervous look on his face, it was almost funny.

We presented ourselves to Mr. Langley at nine o'clock sharp. His face looked puffy like Dad's did when he had a big problem.

"Margaret, Bill, come in and sit down," he said. "I have good news." He looked straight at me. I couldn't even blink. "The computer is being fixed."

"I'm glad to hear that," I whispered.

"Of course, the terminal is covered by a service contract so nobody has to pay the three hundred dollars for the repairs."

"Three hundred dollars?" Bill said.

"Yes. The computer is a complex, expensive machine."

"I'm sorry about the whole thing, Mr. Langley," I said.

"I am, too. Classes will resume as usual tomorrow morning. We'll have to work hard to make up for the lost time." He stood up so I knew the interview was over. I had expected a longer lecture.

"And Margaret . . ."

"Yes?"

"Don't bring your boyfriend to the computer room any more."

"I won't. Thanks, Mr. Langley." I slid out the door. Bill followed, his face red and his eyes bugging out of his head.

"Well, that's good news." Bill seemed surprised.

"I feel I should pay the repair bill," I said. We crossed the sandy parking lot and got into the car.

"I feel responsible, too," Bill said. "I was in a crummy mood that day."

When I got home, Frost was waiting for me on the porch steps. I told him what Mr. Langley had said.

"Well, that puts you in the clear. I'm glad," he said.

"I'm not in the clear. I just don't have to pay

72

the repairs. We still broke the computer," I said.

"Not really, it was my fault."

"Fine. I wish Mr. Langley thought so. He'll probably never ask me to help teach another course."

"Sure he will. You're good at it, aren't you? Accidents happen. You can't go on blaming yourself."

"He did say never to bring my boyfriend to the computer room again." I grinned at him.

"I think he's got something there." Frost stroked his chin like Sherlock Holmes when he's on to a clue.

"I still think I should pay them the money," I said.

"Nonsense. That's what the service contracts are for. Your teacher told you the amount so you would be more careful," Frost argued.

Frost had a windsurfing lesson, so we said good-bye. I put on my swimming suit and hurried out to the Gulf. It was hot and muggy, and there was no hint of a breeze. I swam like a maniac dolphin on an exercise spree. I knew I could swim forever now that the big weight had been lifted from my shoulders. So much for my computer experience for the summer. Four more days and it was time to get back to having fun, enjoying Frost, and becoming more outgoing and popular like Janie.

I could see Nancy plodding through the sand. She grinned at me. "Well, what's the verdict? It's good news, isn't it?"

"How did you know?" I asked.

"You don't swim like that when you're upset."

I laughed. Then I told her what happened with Mr. Langley.

"Janie's coming home Sunday," I said.

"I suppose you're going to spend the rest of the week worrying about that. Honestly, Margaret . . ."

"You know how they act when they get back from cheerleading camp," I protested.

"Phoney up to their eyebrows," Nancy said.

"You don't have to live with Janie," I argued. "She'll be the worst."

"So think about something else." Nancy always had good advice. "You can't change Janie. You can only change yourself."

When we went in, I called Bill and Frost. I hoped they were free Saturday. If they both felt so responsible for the computer accident, maybe they could help me look for shells for a day. There had to be some way I could repay Mr. Langley for being so nice. I could buy him a wedding present. Surely he'd have to accept it. He hadn't lectured me, and that was my definition of a pretty nice guy.

* * * * *

"Margaret, you didn't tell me he was going to be here," Bill snapped, as Frost drove up all smiles on Saturday morning.

"You didn't ask," I said.

"That's false advertising." Bill's eyes flashed.

"You agreed to help me raise the money, didn't you? Are you going to make trouble, or are you going to help hunt for shells?"

"Okay, okay . . . I was surprised, that's all."

"It's a fine day for shelling, right Bill? Did you bring your ant repellent, Margaret?" Frost strutted more than usual when Bill was around.

"If you two would load this gear in the trunk, we could go now," I said.

"Where are we going?" Bill asked.

"Captiva," I said.

"Why waste time driving all the way over there? Let's stay on Sanibel," Bill said.

"We did all right on Captiva the last time," Frost argued. "It was more private there, until the ants came along and spoiled our party." He emphasized "private." Bill's lower lip trembled.

"Okay, let's stay on Sanibel," I said. "If we have a poor morning, we can go to Captiva this afternoon. Let's get started."

We drove to the northern tip of the island where the tourists seldom go. Bill sat in the back seat as nervous as when we were going to hear Mr. Langley's verdict.

"How's this spot?" Frost asked.

"Fine," I said.

Frost parked the car by swerving off the road and screeching to a stop, spraying sand behind him like a vapor trail. Bill turned white. Frost had never driven like this before.

"Here we are." Frost grinned.

We trudged out to the beach, carrying our pails. We stood for a minute blinking in the brilliant sunlight. The contrast between Bill and Frost as they searched for shells was funny. Bill wore a wide-brimmed straw hat with a red and white striped ribbon on it and dark sun glasses. His movements imitated the sand crabs. He was all arms and legs scurrying sideways in search of shells tumbling about in the waves. Frost wore a yellow bathing suit. He stood tall and combed the shallow water slowly, shuffling his feet as I had taught him.

Every time I found a perfect shell, I mentally chalked up its value. Pretty soon my mind became boggled by the numbers. I switched back to watching Bill and Frost. Boys were more fun to think about anyway.

"Hey, look! Dophins . . . a whole school of

them." Bill pointed south.

"Are you sure they're not sharks," Frost teased.

"Of course, I'm sure. I've lived around the ocean all my life," Bill snapped.

"Stop it, you two," I said.

We ate our lunch in uneasy silence. Then we went on with our back-breaking work.

"Margaret, let me empty your bucket," Bill offered. He glanced over at Frost to see if he were watching. Carrying our two pails full of shells, Bill started down the beach toward the car.

"Hey, Bill, look at the shark," Frost yelled.

Bill spun around, was tripped up by a big wave, and went tumbling into the surf. The buckets of shells went flying.

"Frost, look what you've done," I shrieked.

"I'm sorry. I was just teasing," Frost said.

Bill was purple with rage. He stomped off to the car without a word.

"I think I've had enough shelling for one day," Frost announced.

"I've had it, too," I said. "A little cooperation from you two might have made a difference."

We rode back to my house in steamy silence and unloaded the car. Bill rode off on his bicycle without even saying good-bye.

While I was getting steamed up about boys

in general, Frost was standing there with a silly grin on his face.

"What are you grinning about?" I asked. "Why don't you take off, too?"

He leaned back on his elbows on the porch steps and crossed his long legs at the ankle. "Aw, don't be mad at me. I'm sorry I can't get along with your friend, but his pickiness gets to me. He's so easy to tease."

I tried to frown, but it came out more like a smile.

"Let's chalk today up to experience and be friends," he said.

It was hard to resist his smile. "All right," I said. I sat down on the step beside him.

"I wish you would let me give you the money for the gift," he whispered as he put his arm around me. "It was partially my fault about the computer."

"No, I can't take money from you." I shook my head. I couldn't believe he was bringing up the money again.

"Forget it," I said, and I ran into the house. I took the longest shower in history, knowing he wouldn't be there when I got out.

Eleven

THE next day, I escaped the house early for a swim. When I emerged from the Gulf, I saw Frost zigzagging toward me. He was carrying something that looked like a carpet sweeper my grandmother used to have. It had a long handle with a box at the end.

"It's a metal detector," he said, grinning at me.

"Yes, I figured that out," I said.

"With this-here gadget, I'm going to find you a fortune, ma'am." Frost affected a country accent. "Your money problems are over."

"You never give up, do you?" I laughed.

"Tain't in my nature to give up, ma'am." He made an exaggerated bow.

"Are you an actor at heart, or do you really have nine personalities?" I asked.

"I ain't rightly sure, but I did have the role of Cornelius in the high school production of *Hello, Dolly*." He did a little tap dance on the sand.

"Frost, you never told me."

"You never asked." He turned off his gadget and sat down.

"What other secrets are you keeping from me?" I sat down beside him.

"Nothing much. Do I have a deal?"

"What deal?"

"You will not worry about the wedding present until we have had a chance to hunt for our fortune with the metal detector?"

"All right," I agreed.

The hardest part of treasure hunting was dividing the beach into imaginary squares so we could keep track of where we were going. The metal detector was heavy and awkward. Wandering about the beach with one outstretched arm was not my idea of fun.

"Oh, I found something!" I exclaimed.

"What is it?" Frost asked eagerly.

"It's only a quarter. At this rate do you realize how long it will take to find fifty dollars?"

"No. How long?"

"We need two hundred quarters, and we find one every fifteen minutes. You figure it out."

"You're the mathematician, oh practical one. I don't even think in such terms." He spoke with a French accent and twirled an imaginary mustache.

"What makes you think this scheme will work?" I demanded.

"Luck, my dear. Lady Luck will smile on me, and I will find something of great value," he drawled. "I don't expect to pile up many quarters."

"Hmmm . . ." was all I could say. Frost was some kind of thinker when it came to money.

We hunted a little longer, but all we came up with were more quarters and an occasional dime to break the monotony.

"I'm hungry," I said after my stomach had growled for the fifth time.

"It's one-thirty . . . past lunch time," Frost observed, looking at his watch.

"I have to go in. Janie's coming home today. Why don't you stay for lunch?"

"Sounds good."

We left the back-breaking gadget by the steps and went into the house. It seemed dark in the house after the glare of the sun on the sand. Frost placed our quarters in piles on the kitchen table while I made tuna fish sandwiches.

"Four dollars and eighty-five cents," Frost announced proudly.

"That's about seventy-five cents an hour," I said.

"You always look on the dark side of the coin," he teased. "Tomorrow is another day."

"I hope so," I said, without much conviction.

Frost didn't hang around until Janie came home. Mom and Dad had gone to Ft. Myers to pick her up. When she came bursting into the living room, her eyes all aglow, she looked every inch a cheerleader. It was eerie in a way. The living room became the bleachers and Janie, the star.

"Margaret, I missed you so," Janie squealed.

"I missed you, too," I said.

"Wait until you see all the new cheers I've learned. I can't wait to show them to you." As she talked, her hands and arms were working at right angles to her body in a jerky, disjointed fashion. She recited cheers under her breath.

"Didn't they teach you to speak up so we can understand what you say?" Dad asked.

"Everybody talks like this," Janie said. "We learned this really neat 'hello' cheer. Let me show you."

She launched into a louder version with larger scale motions. I could hardly believe Janie was my sister. She looked like an alien robot with its talking button jammed in the "on" position. When she finished, she jumped up in the air and clapped for herself. That showed a lot of spirit, she said.

"Very nice, dear," Mom said, clapping.

"It was great, Janie," I said. I could see I was going to run out of superlatives if this kept up.

"Do you think you can jump up and down like that for three hours straight?" Dad asked, smiling.

"If the football players can run and fall on each other for three hours, I guess I can jump up and down," Janie answered, her eyes sparkling. She impetuously gave Dad a hug. "I missed you," she said.

"By the way, Mom, I invited the girls over on Tuesday to practice," Janie said, draping her arm around Mom's shoulder. "Is it all right?"

"Sure, that's fine," Mom said, hugging her back.

"Would you fix lunch for us, too?" Janie asked.

Mom smiled.

"I guess we can find something," she said.

It sounded like trouble to me. Listening to Janie cheer all the time was one thing, but enduring six bouncing girls added up to pure torture.

Mom served cake and ice cream in honor of Janie's coming home. Janie began her day by day description of camp. Of course I was overjoyed to hear the lowdown on a million girls I didn't even know.

"You should have seen Carrie," Janie said. "She got 'best form' award at the end of the week. I knew she would."

"Who got 'most talkative'? You?" I teased.

"Very funny. But guess what I did get?" Janie purred.

"I can't imagine."

"I got 'most spirited,'" she said proudly.

"That's wonderful, Janie. I'm very proud of you," Mom said.

"Does that mean you're really a ghost?" I asked. Dad laughed and put his arm around me.

"If I am, I'm the ghostest with the mostest," Janie said with a giggle.

Forget any normal conversations with Janie. I knew we were going to live and breathe cheerleading around here whether we liked it or not. She hadn't mentioned boys since she got home. That had to be a first.

Twelve

"THERE you are, me pretty." Frost twirled his imaginary mustache.

"Captain Bluebeard, I presume," I said.

"Are we ready to hunt ze treasure?"

"Ready."

We had chosen the group of motels near the entrance to the island because the most affluent tourists stayed here. We had our searching operation down to the least number of motions now. One rested while the other hunted. Frost went first, and I walked along beside him.

"Still think we'll find our fortune?" I asked.

"It has been done before," Frost pointed out. "Why not us?" Frost was weaving from side to side with his metal box.

"Janie's home from camp," I said.

"How did she like it?"

"She loved it. She cheers from morning till night. If you talk about something else, she stares straight ahead blankly."

"A clear case of cheerleaderitis. I've seen it before."

"You have?"

"Sure. It happens to all the girls."

Just then the metal detector went crazy. The lights flashed, and the buzzer sounded worse than Janie with her volume turned up.

"What's the matter with it?" I said.

"There's something big down there." Frost dug around in the sand. "Here. Hold this thing so I can locate it."

I took the machine and pinpointed the loudest buzz.

"I've got it," he said. "Wow! Paydirt. It's a Rollex watch. Our money problems are over. I can't believe it."

"What's such a big deal about a watch?" I said.

"It's not just a watch. It's a Rollex. They sell for about nine thousand dollars. We can get at least fifteen hundred out of it. That takes care of your wedding gift with plenty to spare. What do you think of this machine now?" He dusted the sand off the watch and handed it to me.

"Nine thousand dollars? That's a lot of money for a watch." I examined it closely. It was beautiful. It was a man's watch with a gold expansion band and a gold face.

"Frost, what if someone lost this watch?

Think how terrible they would feel."

"Of course, someone lost it. People don't throw away expensive watches. Don't worry, it's insured."

"But look, there's an inscription." I turned the watch over and read, "To George from Alice with love, July 12, 1980."

"Let me see." Frost read the inscription.

"It has sentimental value. Maybe we should try to return it," I said.

"Margaret, I can't believe you. You're in a tizzy about paying money back to the school that they won't accept anyway. Then you want to buy a wedding gift. Now when the money for the gift is in your hands, you want to give it back."

"We don't have the money in our hands. We have a watch," I reasoned. " . . . someone else's watch."

"I'm trying to help you, Margaret. Why is it there's always something wrong with the way I try to help you?"

I hesitated, my heart pounding. We were getting involved in an argument about all sorts of issues besides the watch.

"Frost, let's forget about your helping me and . . . "

"Let's forget it, all right. Let's forget that I helped you break the computer. Let's forget that we even know each other." His face was red and his eyes, hurt and angry. He picked up his metal detector and stomped off.

What did I say? I wondered, my head spinning. The argument was all wrong.

Frost turned around and came back, still frowning. "Here." He shoved the watch into my hand. "It's yours. You find the owner if you can."

"But, Frost, I don't want to fight with you," I pleaded, running after him. "I just feel . . . "

"What about how I feel?" His voice was shaky. "Forget it," he said and stomped away again.

This time I let him go. There was no point in fighting when we were upset. How did we get into such a big fight? Who wanted to cash in on a watch that said, "To George from Alice?" Frost did, and I didn't.

The first problem I had was to get Frost on my side without any further bad scenes. My second problem was to find the owner of the watch. If I had lost an expensive watch, what would I do to recover it? I'd probably look in the lost and found section of the newspaper, I thought.

Janie appeared on the path. "Mom wants you," she said in between reciting her cheers.

"What does she want?" I asked.

Janie paused. "Isn't that silly? I can't remember. But I think it was important." She went up the path, swinging her arms and whispering to herself.

Of course it's silly, you cheering zombie, I thought. When are you going to come back to the real world? I silently collected myself and followed her to the house.

"What's up, Mom?" I asked.

"Have you forgotten you have to babysit for Mrs. Jenkins today?" Mom was folding clothes from the dryer.

"Gosh, I did forget." I glanced at the clock. "I only have ten minutes to shower and get there."

"What about lunch?" Mom called.

"I'll have something over there," I called back from the bathroom. Frost could have his watch, I thought. With a few more babysitting jobs like this one, I could buy my own wedding present.

* * * * *

Early the next day Janie's friends invaded the place with their Crest smiles and motorized arms and legs. Each arrived in matching shorts and tops and an assortment of braids and other bizarre hair styles.

Frost was waiting for me at the beach when I escaped from the pack. "What have you decided about the watch?"

No good morning, I thought. No funny impersonations, no warmth . . . just what did I want to do with the watch?

"Good morning," I smiled sweetly, taking my cue from all the smiles I had witnessed in the house.

"Margaret, I can't figure you out."

"Frost, I can't figure you out either," I said. I decided on a frontal attack.

"What do you mean?"

"How would you feel if you lost a nine thousand dollar watch. Maybe the owner lost his job and has six starving children. He could sell the watch to feed his children . . . if he had the watch."

"You're fantasizing, Margaret. That's my department."

"I knew you'd say something like that."

"So what are you going to do about the watch?" We were back where we started.

"How about a compromise? Let's put an ad in the lost and found section and see what happens," I suggested.

"Okay, if you don't locate the owner within three days, we keep the watch. Deal?"

"Deal." I felt triumphant. We had reached an agreement without a bad scene.

Suddenly my soaring feeling came to a screeching halt. I could see Janie and her friends approaching. "Want to go for a walk?"

I asked Frost. But it was too late. They had seen us.

"Frost, how are you?" Janie was gushy.

"Hi, Janie, how was camp?" He grinned at her.

"Marvelous. Do you know Carrie? She's a cheerleader," Janie shrieked in her excited professional voice.

The phrase caught on. "Hi, I'm Debbie, and I'm a cheerleader." They all laughed.

"Hi, I'm Jean, and I'm a cheerleader." And so on. I was getting nauseous.

"Let's show Frost a cheer," Debbie suggested.

"Right." They all clapped.

Sweat formed on my upper lip. I felt hot and sticky and embarrassed. How could they jump up and down in the hot sun and still look gorgeous? And Frost was even worse. He was making a fool out of himself just watching.

"Hey, that was great," he said.

"Where's Allen?" I asked. "I thought he was coming over."

"He'll be here after football practice," Janie said.

The girls were asking Frost how old he was. I felt invisible. There was no way I could get Frost away from them until the boys showed up. Fortunately the girls got hot and decided to go swimming.

"Now don't you go away, Frost," Janie's voice rang out. "You're just what we need to critique our cheers."

Frost pulled at my hand. When we had slipped away, I realized I had a sick smile pasted on my face.

"Disgusting," I said aloud.

"Don't be too hard on them," Frost said. "They're just having a good time."

"Yeah," I said.

"Didn't you ever want to be a cheerleader? Now be honest?"

"Every girl wants to be a cheerleader in ninth grade. But I got over it."

"These girls deserve the applause. Look how hard they've worked already."

"Do you like cheerleader types?" I asked, looking at him.

"I like your type, Margaret." Frost grinned at me. I was positively glowing inside.

We took only a short walk because I had to go to work. From the store I phoned in the information about the watch. The caller would have to identify the watch by the inscription. Otherwise anyone could claim it. If the ad failed to find the owner, then the watch would be ours.

Thirteen

THE ad ran for three days without results. The next morning Frost was waiting at our usual spot.

"Does the jury have the verdict?" he asked in mock seriousness.

I smiled. We both knew I hadn't located the owner of the watch. "Here's the watch. No luck."

"Case dismissed by reason of no owner," Frost declared.

"And what do we do with the evidence, Your Honor?" I asked.

"I'll take care of that. We'll have plenty of money soon. Your troubles are over, madame."

"What are you going to do with the rest of the money?" I asked.

"I don't know. What shall we do with it?"

"It's your money. I don't want it," I said hurriedly.

"There you go trying to give it away again."

I grinned. "I guess you're right."

"How about an ice cream cone to celebrate?" he suggested.

"All right."

We went through the house to pick up my purse. Before we got out the front door, the telephone rang. I answered it.

"Is this the party that advertised finding a Rollex watch?" a man's voice asked.

"Yes," I said.

"This is George Early. I lost my watch a few days ago."

My heart did a double lurch when he said "George." "We're asking callers to identify the inscription," I said.

"Yes, I understand. My watch says, 'To George from Alice with love, July 12, 1980.' "

"My gosh." I covered the mouthpiece. "It's the owner."

Frost grinned and shrugged. "So give him his watch."

"Mr. Early?" I said. "We found your watch."

Mr. Early was a nice little old man whose wife had died a few months ago. He was happy to get the watch back because his wife had given it to him. Mr. Early had insisted on giving us a fifty dollar reward for returning the watch. I didn't want to take it, but he wouldn't hear of our not accepting it.

When we left, I had a lump in my throat. "It's too bad people have to go through life so lonely," I said to Frost.

"Yeah, he sure misses his wife."

"Aren't you glad we found the owner now that you've met Mr. Early?" I asked, watching his face.

"Yes, Margaret, you were right. Insurance can't cover everything." He smiled at me.

We walked across the street to the ice cream parlor. I ordered one scoop of chocolate and one scoop of pistachio. Frost got two scoops of butter pecan.

"We'll buy a nice present for your teacher with the reward money," Frost said.

"Hmmm . . ." I appeared to be thinking it over. Actually my ice cream was dripping, and I could either eat it or let the chocolate drip on my white shorts.

"And there's only one thing to do with the money that's left over," Frost declared.

"What?" I asked.

"Let's have lunch at the Sand Dunes one more time."

"It's a deal," I said, shaking his hand across the table.

* * * * *

We got all dressed up to go to the Sand Dunes again. This time I wore less makeup. I couldn't stand the stuff really. It made me feel like I was wearing a mask.

Frost wore a tan summer suit and a white

shirt with a narrow tan stripe in it. His shirt opened at the neck.

I wore my lavender dress. I thought it made me look too young because it had so many ruffles. But I didn't have anything else to wear. I must have looked all right, though, because Frost kept staring at me.

We didn't talk much. There was a magical mood between us that we both understood. Talking was much overrated anyway.

Frost pulled up to the entrance gate and stopped. He grinned at me and waited for Gus to come out. What a surprise when someone other than Gus emerged from the building. His name tag read, "Charlie."

"Can I help you kids?" His voice was raspy.

"Ah, yes, I'm Frost Duvall. My father, A.L. Duvall, is selling the Hidden Cove Condominium group farther up the island. Miss Halton and I have had lunch in your dining room before," Frost began.

Charlie took forever reading the names on his clip board. "I'm sorry. You're not on the list."

"Would you please call your office and see if we could get clearance?" Frost requested.

Charlie hesitated. "All right."

"What bad luck. No Gus," I said when Charlie went back inside to call.

"I should have checked it out first," Frost said.

Charlie came back out, frowning. "Sorry. We need a phone call ahead of time."

"Thanks." Frost turned the car around and started home. The drive was just as beautiful from this direction, but some of the magic had disappeared.

"We could eat at one of the other hotels," I said.

"Wouldn't be the same." Frost stared straight ahead.

"Let's not let it spoil our day," I insisted. "Think of something else fun to do."

"I'll take you to my favorite place," Frost said, suddenly making a right turn.

"Where is that?"

He pulled up to the island hot dog stand. "Stay right here."

I couldn't figure out his logic this time. I'd spent an hour ironing my best dress for a hot dog stand? He came back with two large hot dogs with everything and two large Cokes in a paper bag.

"Hold this," he said, smiling.

Frost drove the two blocks between the hot dog stand and Mom's shop. "Here it is," he said as we got out of the car, "my favorite place."

I was one big question mark. "Mom's shop is your favorite place to have lunch?"

"Yes," Frost said. "I met you here." He opened the door and smiled at me. I smiled back. We walked into the shop hand in hand.

"Hi, guys," Janie called from behind the cash register.

Frost looked at Janie, his eyes all aglow. She looked at him the same way. A burning started in my heart and traveled down to consume all my insides.

"Janie doesn't have a hot dog," I said.

Frost eyed me strangely. "I'll go and get her one."

He left and Janie started her motorized legs and arms. "I love working on slow days," she said. "I get in lots of cheering practice."

I took an uneven breath. "Yeah." I watched Janie's whole repertoire of cheers. I was trying to convince myself that Frost's smile was for me and not her. But I wasn't getting very far.

"I thought you and Frost were having lunch at the Sand Dunes," Janie said.

"They wouldn't let us in," I said.

"How nasty of them."

"Who's nasty?" Frost asked, bringing in a hot dog, dripping with the fixings.

"Those old condominium people were nasty not to let you in," Janie pouted.

"See what they missed out on." He gestured to me.

"Of course." Janie giggled.

She was pouring on the charm all right. Her eyes practically never left his face. It was murder to watch. It was strange how sure of myself and sure of Frost I felt when we were alone. But when we were with Janie, I wasn't sure of anything. Maybe I was crazy. No normal person could have such changeable opinions about herself.

"Margaret, you haven't eaten your hot dog," Frost observed.

At least he noticed me. "I'm not hungry," I said.

Come on, you have to get over this, I thought, giving myself a silent pep talk. Janie likes Allen Patten. Janie likes Allen Patten.

"Where's Allen today, Janie?" I asked.

"I haven't the foggiest," Janie said. "But Frost is here to keep me company."

My insides were still burning and my knees were beginning to weaken. Eating was out of the question. I had to leave.

"Frost, we'd better go," I said.

"What's your hurry? I'm still eating." He and Janie were discussing which brands of boardsails were the best.

I thought about getting sick. No, a frontal attack would be better. I waited until Frost finished eating.

"I have to go home now," I said. They both looked at me as if I'd just said, "I want my mommy."

"All right," Frost said. "See you, Janie."

"Bye, Frost. Bye, Margaret. Thanks for the lunch." Janie's words danced around the store.

"What's the matter, Margaret?" Frost asked. "I thought having lunch in the store would be romantic."

"It's not romantic with three people," I snapped.

"Are you still jealous of Janie? I thought we settled that long ago." The car screeched around the corner.

"Did I say Janie? No, I said three people. Now who's jumping to conclusions." I think I was shouting.

"Calm down, will you? Janie flirts with everybody. That's the way she is. It doesn't mean anything."

"It depends on who's watching." The tears dripped on my hand. I tried to ignore them.

"I'm sorry, Margaret. But it's a little impossible for me never to see Janie. She is your sister."

"Forget it."

"No, I don't want to forget it. Not talking about it won't solve anything."

"Well, I don't want to talk about it any more." He had reached the driveway. I got out, slammed the door, and ran into the house.

I watched Frost drive away and immediately wished he were back again. I wanted to explain what I meant. I thought I was going crazy. I felt so mixed up. Maybe I'd wait awhile and then call him. I'd apologize for getting so upset.

Fourteen

WHEN Allen showed up that evening to take Janie to the movies, I still felt confused.

"I'll be out in a sec," Janie called.

"How's football practice?" I tried to think of something to say to him.

"It's easier now that I'm in shape."

I laughed. "So now you're in shape, huh?"

"Sure I am. Look at this." He flexed his biceps for me.

"Ooh, I'm impressed," I giggled.

"Come on," he said, dancing around on his feet like a fighter. "Hit me in the stomach. Bet you hurt your hand. Come on, hit me."

"You're on." I faked a couple of punches like I'd seen the guys do, and then I landed one on his stomach. His muscles were solid and didn't give a fraction of an inch.

"Hey, you have toughened up." I rubbed my hand.

"What'd I tell you?" He grinned smugly.

"Allen, may I ask you a question?" I said,

in a more serious tone.

"Sure."

"Do you ever get jealous when Janie flirts with another boy?"

He frowned a little in pain or maybe embarrassment. "No, Janie is Janie. Some guys try to change their girl friends. But I never went in for all that possessive garbage. Janie and I have a good time going out. Why mess it up?"

Janie walked in before I could comment. "My, you two seem pretty serious." Her words didn't dance around the room.

"I was asking Allen his advice."

"I see. Well, let's go Allen. The movie starts at seven-thirty." She took his arm and walked him out the door. Allen waved good-bye, which was as much as he had time to do.

Was Janie jealous of me talking to Allen? I wondered. I laughed out loud. Maybe it went with the territory, being jealous. If you cared for someone as much as I cared for Frost, maybe being jealous was natural. What a terrible way to pay for the caring.

* * * * *

Frost came over the next morning early. He couldn't stay mad for long, I realized.

"Margaret, about yesterday . . . I'm sorry

our plans didn't work out. I understand how it must have looked to you."

"I'm sorry, too. I guess I overreacted."

Frost looked relieved. He seemed excited about something. Now that the fight was resolved, he grinned. "I've got something to show you. Come on. Bring what you'll need for the day."

"What about lunch?" I asked.

"I brought lunch. Wear your swimming suit."

"Okay," I said, smiling. "Just give me a minute or two."

I hurried to change my clothes. When I came back out, Frost grabbed my hand and pulled me in the direction of the beach. He ran ahead and then turned to watch my reaction.

Frost had stopped beside a brand new boat. It was a small white runabout with red cushions and a red stripe around the side. A shiny black outboard motor tilted up out of the shallow water. The little boat rocked gently in the waves.

"Wow, Frost, it's a beauty." I walked all around it.

Frost beamed. "I knew you'd like it. Dad gave it to me for my birthday."

"Your birthday? You didn't tell me it was your birthday," I shrieked. "Don't say it. I didn't ask you. You're seventeen, right?"

"Right."

"What did your mom say about the boat?"

"She's not thrilled, but she'll get over it. Come on, I'll take you for a ride."

"I'd love to. But Mom isn't home. I should let her know."

"You could call her."

"She's not at the store yet." I hesitated. "Maybe I'll just leave a note."

I ran back to the house. I felt a little guilty about taking off. But since it was Frost's birthday, I knew Mom would understand. I wrote a short note and dashed out to the beach. Frost had hauled anchor and was idling the motor.

"Hurry up. I'm getting carried out by the tide," Frost called.

"I'm coming." I raced through the waves and climbed in.

"It's so beautiful . . . so new and shiny. They don't stay that way long in the salt water. Most of the boats I've seen are old and weather-beaten." I felt my way around the boat, peering at every gadget. I touched the textured canvas of the cushions and felt the smooth fiberglass hull.

Frost grinned at my delight as he maneuvered the boat out beyond the waves. "Guess what I'm going to name her?"

"What?" I sat on the red cushion next to the

driver's seat, looking straight at Frost.

"Guess. I'm not going to tell."

"Let's see. Aphrodite."

"Afro-what?"

"Aphrodite, the goddess of beauty."

"Nope, I'm going to name her Margaret." His eyes twinkled.

"Oh, Frost, how sweet." I gave him a hug and a big kiss on the cheek.

"Ooops!" He angled to the left to avoid side-swiping a channel marker. "Not while I'm driving, Margaret."

I giggled. I watched the island from the Gulf. What a different view it was than from the land. The presence of all the live oak trees made the island look mysterious and a tiny bit foreboding. Yet the land was home, cozy and familiar.

"Where are we going?" I asked.

"How about Captiva?" Frost suggested. "I've been wanting to go back there."

"That sounds great. I see you've even brought buckets for shells."

"We skirted the shore of Captiva, which looked even more foreboding than Sanibel because it had fewer inhabitants.

"Look for a good place to anchor," Frost said.

I nodded. "How about over there?" I pointed to a beach with lots of sand and fewer trees. It looked inviting.

Frost cut the engine and glided in slowly. When the bow slid onto the sand, I hopped out, carrying the anchor. I dug it into the sand as solidly as I could. Frost handed the lunch and pails over to me. After he got out, he pushed the boat farther up on the sand and then tightened the anchor rope.

"With the tide going out, you can't be too careful," he explained. "Anchors have been known to pull loose and be dragged out to sea with the boat."

"How did a landlubber like you know that?"

"Dad made me take a boating safety course before he would buy the boat."

"Another one of those things I forgot to ask you?" I teased.

"I wanted it to be a surprise."

The beach was one of the most beautiful spots I had ever seen. A few craggy rocks protuded into the sea, causing the waves to spray into the air like a natural fountain. The sand was fine and white, a perfect spot for shelling.

Frost watched me. "I see shells in your eyes."

"Yes, but no red ants, thank you."

"Just stay out of the woods, Margaret."

He handed me a pail. I began my slow, careful shuffle. It didn't take long to make an exciting discovery. "It's the season for olive shells," I announced.

"What do you mean?"

There are thousands of these shells on the beach right now." I held up a handful of the shiny, capsule-shaped shells.

"They're very pretty," Frost commented.

"The markings always remind me of hieroglyphics," I said. "All the shells seem to wash up on the beaches in seasons. But it's not a yearly thing so I'm never sure what shells I'll find and when I'll find them."

"They should learn to make reservations," Frost said, waving an imaginary cigar and raising his eyebrows a la Groucho Marx.

I smiled. "Come on. We can't let all the olive shells slip away from us."

"Yes, ma'am." Frost saluted me, picked up his pail, and marched down the beach.

We worked hard all morning. We plucked handfuls of shells out of the waves only to have two more handfuls take their place. The buckets filled, and my back began to ache and feel slightly sunburned.

"Water." Frost staggered toward me like a man in a desert movie. "If I don't get a drink I'm done for."

"Let's break for lunch," I said. I handed him a Coca-cola out of the cooler.

"After lunch I'm going swimming," Frost

declared. "I don't care how much of a slave driver you are."

"Me, too," I said.

We ate and then stretched our muscles in the warm water.

"Ahhh . . . " Frost sighed happily.

"I agree. It feels divine."

The water was so clear we could see our toes. Frost dove underwater and made faces at me. He was so funny I laughed until my sides ached.

"I have to leave for home next week," Frost said while we were resting on the sand.

"Oh, no," I groaned. "You shouldn't have told me today."

"Orlando is only five hours away," he said. "Maybe you can come up and visit."

"I'd like to," I said. "Can't you come back here for visits, too? How about Thanksgiving, Christmas, and Spring vacation?"

"I'll try," he said. "Will you promise to write?"

"This is a depressing conversation." I stood up and grabbed my pail. "Come on, the olive shells wait for no man or woman."

"I'm not moving until you promise to write to me." He folded his arms across his chest.

I knelt beside him. "Of course, I'll write to you." My eyes filled with tears. "I don't want to think about your leaving until I have to."

He hugged me, and I hugged him back. Then he stood up. "You are interfering with my work, madame. My boss won't like it at all." He tried to be funny, and I tried to laugh. It was hard with a lump in my throat.

Frost put the lunch cooler back in the boat and picked up his pail. The work was tedious and not nearly as much fun as it had been in the morning. Why did Frost have to remind me? What a way to spoil a perfect day. A distant rumble of thunder interrupted my darkening mood.

"Did you hear that?" Frost asked.

"I heard it." I scanned the dark clouds in the Northwest. The darkness of the clouds formed a straight line down to the horizon. It was raining on the Gulf.

"The rain will reach us in about a half hour," I said.

"Let's head back," Frost said. "I don't want to get caught in the rain."

"It might blow over. These afternoon storms never last long."

"Yes, but it might not. Let's go."

I started the engine while Frost hauled anchor and pushed the boat into the water. The wind was brisker, and the boat was tossed around by the waves. We eased out into the channel and started for Sanibel. The thunder bellowed again. It was accompanied by jagged lines of glowing lightning.

"It's going to rain sooner than I thought," I said. "The wind is bringing it in fast."

"Thanks for the weather report," Frost growled.

"Hey, don't get ugly with me," I retorted.

"I'm sorry, Margaret. But it scares me to be bouncing around on the ocean during bad weather."

"Don't panic, I can handle a boat."

"Thanks, that makes me feel very safe." The sarcasm in his voice was as biting as the wind which stung my face and whipped through my hair. I couldn't figure him out. He had never acted like this before.

Frost tried to steer the boat into the waves, but they seemed to be going in all directions. I tried to point out the larger, white-capped waves. The spray stung our eyes and our skin. It even seemed hard to breathe in the salt-sticky wetness. Frost jammed the throttle forward. The boat lunged ahead, slapping hard against the choppy water. I held on tight.

The clouds were completely black now. Huge raindrops plopped down for about thirty seconds, and then it poured. The rain pounded against my body like needles. Water blinded me and made it hard for me to breathe. I felt like hiding under the seat. The boat seemed to leap into the air and then fall jarringly onto the churning ocean. I couldn't see land anywhere.

"Windbreakers!" Frost shouted.

"Where?"

"They're under your seat."

I gripped the back of the seat to keep from being swept overboard. I knelt on the floor and raised the cushion. Under the hinged seat were two yellow windbreakers. I grabbed them and handed one to Frost. We struggled into them, taking turns trying to steady the wheel. It was immediate relief. I was still wet, of course, but the pelting against my skin stopped. I felt steamy and warmer inside the waterproof jacket. I hadn't realized how cold I was. My teeth began to chatter in delayed reaction.

"The boat's taking on water," Frost yelled.

I turned around and gaped. The back of the boat was riding low in the water. About four inches of water had accumulated in the stern. I grabbed a pail and began to bail. I was angry at the storm and at Frost for doing nothing. Why had we gone out on the boat without telling anyone where we were going?

No matter how fast I bailed, the water kept coming down in sheets. My back began to ache, and my anger welled up in my throat in sobs and gasps.

"Margaret, it's gaining on you," Frost yelled.

"If you think you can do any better, you do it." I threw the pail at him. He ducked and the plastic pail disappeared in a raging wave.

I froze. If this were a war between the storm and me, the storm would win. The thought had a sobering effect. I grabbed the other pail, emptied the shells overboard, and bailed as hard as I could.

When I felt I could talk to Frost in a calm voice, I asked, "Do you know where we are?"

"No," he said.

It was a stupid question, for there was no land in sight. There was only rain and choppy seas on all sides of us. I kept on bailing, but I began to think about survival. There was no food and nothing left to drink. How soon would our parents start looking for us? How long could we survive until they found us?

We had to take turns bailing. I crawled back to where Frost was. His hands were glued to the steering wheel.

"You bail awhile," I said.

He nodded, but he turned the wheel over to me reluctantly. I tried to hold the boat steady and steer into the waves to prevent them from breaking into the boat and flooding it. Like a zombie, Frost stared at the water in the stern and bailed with quick, jerky motions.

Fifteen

IT was getting dark. The rain had let up a little, but the clouds were still black and rolling. I wished I could call my parents and tell them to come and get me. Probably they were really worried by now.

"Frost, the cooler might have some fresh water."

He quit bailing and opened the cooler. He grinned and held it up to me. There was easily a half gallon of melted ice in there.

"There are some cups in the lunch basket. Don't drink it all at once," I advised.

Frost produced the cups and filled one for me. It was so hard to see in the dark. I grabbed the cup and drank the water down in big gulps.

"Now that the rain has let up, maybe we should drop anchor and wait until morning," Frost said.

"I'm hungry," I said.

"Me, too. But if we keep going, we run the

risk of being stranded farther out in the gulf," he went on.

"I know. I know. I don't know what to do." It irritated me that he was arguing with me.

Frost continued to bail, and I steered at about twenty miles per hour.

I think we should keep going," I said, suddenly.

"Why?"

"If they're searching for us, they might hear the boat's motor. Who knows, we might even go in the right direction," I added hopefully.

"We could run out of gas, too." Frost sat in the bottom of the boat, his arms clasped around his knees. I had never seen him so depressed.

"Well, we have to do something. We can't sit here and wait for the sharks to find us." I turned away from him.

"Margaret, I'm so sorry I got you into this mess." I thought he was going to cry.

"It's not your fault there was a storm," I said, trying to console him.

He didn't say any more, but he didn't move either. I knew I had to do something. I revved up the engine.

"Where are you going?" Frost asked.

"Anywhere. Home." I headed with the waves. The clouds had been coming in when the storm started. If the tides were moving with the clouds, then we might reach the shore. The drizzle stopped. I took that as a good sign. Feeling I was doing the right thing gave me a sudden thrill. I knew I had courage or stupidity, but I wasn't sure which.

We motored steadily. I strained my eyes for a glimmer of light or some sign of land. There was nothing but wet blackness and tossing waves. The wind picked up. I pulled my windbreaker tighter around my ears. It was chilly. I felt depressed. Sometimes it was difficult to stay awake. Frost never moved. I thought he had turned to stone.

"I wish we had a compass," I muttered. "Then getting out of here would be a cinch." I tried to sound confident.

"A compass?" Frost said. "I think there's one under the seat where the windbreakers were."

"You think there's a compass aboard?" I was flabbergasted.

He opened the hinged seat and felt around inside.

"Here's a flashlight," he said.

"Great." I took the flashlight while Frost continued to look for the compass. "Is this it?" Frost produced a tiny, rectangular box. While he held the flashlight, I opened the box.

"A circle with a needle pointing north never looked so beautiful," I said. "Why didn't you think of this before?"

"I don't know." He sat back down on the bottom of the boat.

"Never mind, Frost," I said. "I just thought of it myself."

I set our course for due east, figuring we'd run into land soon. Between the hunger gnawing at my stomach and the motion of the waves, I was slightly nauseous.

"I'm starved," I said.

"So am I," he answered. "What time is it?"

I held my watch up to the dash light. "My gosh, it's two o'clock in the morning."

"I can believe it," he said. Frost checked the cooler for any leftover food. "There isn't even a breadcrumb." I sensed the panic in his voice.

"I see a light!" Frost exclaimed.

"Yes, I see it, too." I changed our course to the southeast and headed for the dim flicker of light.

Just then the motor coughed once and died. "Oh, no," I said.

"What's wrong?" Frost asked.

I directed the beam of the flashlight at the instrument panel. "We're out of gas."

"We can't be." Frost sounded angry now.

"The gauge is on empty. See for yourself." I handed him the flashlight.

"Let me try it once." He took the wheel and turned the key. The motor sputtered, but it didn't start. Frost hit the wheel with his fist.

"Is there a reserve fuel supply for emergencies?"

"No." He turned the key again. The motor started.

"Wow!" I said. "It's a miracle."

"The man told us that the gauge would say 'empty' long before we ran completely out of gas," Frost said.

We reached land and tied up at the nearest dock. We walked on shaky sea legs and with queasy stomachs to the house.

We knocked on the door forever before somebody turned on a flood light. Frost and I blinked at each other. We were too exhausted to comment. An old man peered at us over a chain lock. "What are you kids doing out so late?" the man asked.

"Our boat was blown out in the storm," I answered.

"We'd like to use your phone to call our parents," Frost added.

"Land sakes, Hubert, these children are half starved. Can't you see that?" A woman peered at us from behind her husband. She herded us into her kitchen. I dialed home. Hearing Mom's voice made me feel like crying.

"Margaret, where are you? We've been so worried. Yes, Robert, it's her. She says she's all right."

The lady gave Mom the address while Frost and I began to eat cold fried chicken and bread, butter, and jam. Mom and Dad finally arrived, followed by Frost's parents. There was much hugging and kissing. And there were many tears and questions. "Why didn't you tell us where you were going?" "Why didn't you come home before it started raining?"

After a round of thank-yous, we were on our way down the winding road under the familiar tunnel of live oak trees.

I hadn't said good-bye to Frost. The last thing I remember was his sorrowful face as we got into the cars. But I didn't have the energy to worry about him. I wanted to sleep and forget all about the nightmare on the boat.

Sixteen

I had slept sixteen hours the first night. It was a safe, dreamless sleep. The night-mares came later when I was awake. I'd be sitting there with my eyes open, reliving being on the boat in the storm. I tried to shut out the memories. For the most part I had kept my head in the emergency. But I knew Frost felt he hadn't. I needed to talk to him about it. I wanted to let him know I still believed in him.

"Has Frost called?" I asked.

"No," Mom said. "He's probably recovering, too."

I decided to walk down to the beach. Maybe Frost was waiting for me. When I got there, the beach was deserted. I stared at the sea that had frightened me so much. Today it looked beautiful. It was a calm blue-green.

I didn't feel like swimming. When I got hot, I went up to the house and took a shower. I stretched out on my bed. There were only four more days until Frost would leave. Why hadn't he called? Maybe he was really sick. Maybe he never wanted to see me again.

Janie burst through the door with typical cheerleader energy. "Hey, what's wrong? Lose your best friend?"

"I'm just tired," I said.

"You'll get over it. How's Frost these days? Has he recovered from your big adventure?" She blinked her eyes so self-assuredly I wondered what she would do in a real emergency.

"I don't know," I said.

"Frost needs time to get over it, too. Just think, he must feel twice as bad because he didn't get to be the hero."

"You really think that's it?"

"Sure. All boys are like that. They want to protect us girls." She strutted off to the shower.

How did she do it? She was so good at figuring people out. I muddled along not knowing my own mind, let alone what somebody else thought. Janie was probably right. Frost was pouting because he felt responsible and hadn't acted like the big hero. He didn't have to feel that way on my account. Nobody expected him to be superman, especially not me. I only had four days to convince him.

Janie emerged from the shower and went

into the kitchen. I heard her dial the phone. I sneaked down the hall to hear who she was calling.

"Allen, this is Janie. I want to apologize about last night. The argument was my fault."

"No, I insist," Janie went on. "It was my fault. I was making fun of football. That made you lose your temper."

Janie smiled at his answer. "Okay, see you in half an hour."

I stood there dumbfounded. Something important just happened, but I wasn't sure what. Janie hummed a cheer as she bounded toward the bedroom to dress.

"Did you just make up with Allen?" I asked.

"Uh-huh."

"Do you really think the fight was your fault?"

Janie eyed me mysteriously. "It was about half and half. But it doesn't do any good to hold out for complete victory, does it?"

"No, I suppose not."

"Look at it this way, Margaret. If I had waited for Allen to apologize to me, would we be going to the movies in half an hour? No, we'd be wasting our time being mad."

"I see. Excuse me, I've got a call to make." I ran to the phone and dialed Frost's number. There wasn't any answer. I hung up. Why did these things always work for Janie and not for me? I dialed again. Frost answered.

"Hey, you're home," I said.

"Margaret? Did you call before? I was in the shower."

"Oh," I said.

"How are you feeling?" he asked.

"I'm fine now. How are you?"

"Okay. Yeah, I'm fine."

"Frost, I need to talk to you. Can you come over?"

There was a pause. "Are you sure it's all right?" he asked.

"Yes, I'm sure. I'll meet you on the beach."

"I'll be right there," he said. "Margaret? Thanks for calling."

Seventeen

THE sun was almost ready to set when I hurried out to the beach to meet Frost. I had worried away the day, but now I had a solution. Janie was right. Sitting around waiting for something to happen never accomplished anything.

A shiver went up and down my spine. I had learned Janie's secret to popularity, after all. Action was the secret. Janie was popular because she made things happen. She was nice to kids, and they responded. She worked at it.

"Hi, Margaret." Frost stopped in front of me.

I took his arm. "Come on, we have some talking to do."

"I'm not sure I'm ready for this." Frost dug his toes in the sand. "I'm supposed to admit I'm terrible in an emergency. Then I'm supposed to thank you for saving my life."

"Why should you have to say anything like that?"

"How else are we going to resolve this? You know that's why I didn't call you?"

"Yes, but I called you. Doesn't that tell you something?"

"I'm not reading you, Margaret."

"It doesn't matter who did what or how anyone is supposed to act. The important thing is we survived. And I like you just the way you are," I said, stopping to look at him.

He was embarrassed. "That's too easy."

"It's not easy at all." I held both his hands. "We were both worried about how the other felt. We're just people, doing the best we can. There are things about myself I don't like. I always wanted to be more like Janie, the popular one. But you like me the way I am, so please let me like you the way you are."

When he swallowed, his Adam's apple bobbed up and down. "Well, if you aren't the purttiest, silver-tongued she-devil I ever seen," he drawled.

I laughed and flung myself into his arms. Frost swung me around. Then he kissed me, and I kissed him back. Wow! The coral of the sky at sunset had never been so beautiful.

We sat down on the sand and watched the gulls against the setting sun. I felt happy and sad at the same time. We had finally gotten things straightened out, and Frost had to leave in a few days.

"I sold the boat," Frost said.

"You did? Why?"

"Mom insisted. I was lucky to sell it so quickly."

"Yes, you were." I waited.

"I leave tomorrow."

"I thought you had three more days." My heart was beating so fast. It was as if he were fading away from me.

"Dad needs to get back for a meeting."

"Then you were going to leave without calling me?"

"No, Margaret. I'd never do that. I'd planned to come over tonight anyway," he assured me. "It was hard for me to come over, don't you know that?"

"Yes, yes, we've been through that already."

"Will you write to me?" he asked.

"You know I will. You have to promise to write me, too."

"I promise. I want you to visit me, too. Do you think your parents will let you?"

"I think so. If you visit here, too."

"I guess all that's left is saying good-bye," he said, looking at me.

"No, let's not say it yet. Come over tomorrow before you leave."

"I can't. We leave early in the morning."

"Let's pretend you're coming over tomorrow," I said, trying to smile and cover up the wave of panic and sadness that had just hit me.

"You're becoming more like me," he said, laughing.

Then I knew I had to say good night before I started to cry. He kissed me and gave me a long hug.

"I'll call you tomorrow," he said. I watched his long strides down the beach until he was a shadow in the dark.

*　*　*　*　*

"Why were you late to dinner?" Janie asked, in her usual way of getting right to the heart of an issue.

"I went for a walk," I said, in my usual way of side-stepping the issue.

"Frost is leaving tomorrow, huh?" She kept right on track.

"How did you know?"

"His mom told Mom at the store."

"I didn't know you knew Frost's mom."

"You'd know a lot more if you paid attention instead of staying off in that dream world of yours," she scolded.

"Maybe you're right," I said. "Janie, I want to thank you for your advice about Frost. I probably would never have figured out his problem."

"Sure you would," she said. "As smart as you are? I've wished more than once I had your brains."

"You have? That's funny," I said. "I've wished more than once that I were as popular as you are."

"You got your wish this summer. You had two boys fighting over you," Janie said.

"Two boys?"

"Don't play dumb, Margaret. Bill Creamer and Frost Duvall. That's two boys."

"Bill is just my friend."

"Some of the boys I know are just friends, too."

I laughed. I guess I'd accomplished my goal to become more like Janie. The hardest thing was admitting it.

* * * * *

The phone rang at seven-thirty the next morning. "I called to say good-bye," Frost said.

"I'm glad you called," I said. "It's easier over the phone."

He gave me his address. "Say good-bye to Bill for me. Tell him I'm sorry I was so hard on him."

"I'll tell him." My heart was bursting.

"I'm sorry about the computer," Frost said.

127

"It's okay."

"I'm sorry about the boat, too." His voice was thick.

"We already talked about that," I said, gently.

"I know, but I had to say it."

"I know."

"It was a great summer, Margaret. I sure learned a lot."

"I know what you mean," I said. "I learned a lot, too."

"Bye, Margaret. Write soon."

"I will. Bye, Frost."

We hung up at the same time. He hadn't said the words, but I could feel them. He hadn't said he loved me, but we both knew what we felt. It was a summer we'd always remember.